BRADLEY

Gates of Heaven – Book 5

M. Tasia

ALSO BY M. TASIA

The Boys of Brighton series

Gabe

Sam's Soldiers

Rick's Bear

Jesse

Coop

Travis

Grady

Vincent

Shadow

The Holidays

The Gates of Heaven series

Saint

Finn

James

Joey

EVERYONE LOVES
THE BOYS OF BRIGHTON

"I loved this book and I love this town. I hope there's going to be more."
—Melissa Lemons on *Gabe*

"An amazing read that was filled with lust, love, crazy hot sex, danger, action and so much more This is the first book I have read in this series but I will definitely be reading more in the future."
—Gay Book Reviews on *Sam's Soldiers*

"I was crazy impressed that the author made me teary over the ending of a relationship that I shouldn't have even been invested in. I didn't yet know these characters yet the author made me hurt for them. That takes some mad writing skills!"
—Love Bytes Reviews

"Jesse and Royce together have my heart. Jesse has it all by himself."
—The Book Junkie Reads on *Jesse*

"So much action, intrigue, drama and angst for the long awaited story of Grady and Ben. This was worth the wait. Sexy and sweet. I can't wait for the next."
—SamD on *Grady*

"I knew this one would be my favorite to date! There was something about Vincent that said awesome then came Tristan."
—Booky on *Vincent*

"This installment of the Boys of Brighton was so good! I loved Shadow and Randy 's story I was hooked from the first page to the last. This book was definitely worth the wait!"
—AG on *Shadow*

"I have loved this series from the very first story and this holiday novella is simply perfect. We get a glimpse of all our couples and what is happening in their lives while the holidays explode around them. I cannot wait for more!"
—bookobsessed on *The Holidays*

EVERYONE'S NEWEST LOVE
THE GATES OF HEAVEN

"Having read the entire Boys of Brighton series, I was eagerly awaiting Saint's story and it was so worth the wait. I enjoyed every word. I am always amazed by authors that bring characters to life so much that you can hardly wait for the next story. Cannot wait for

Finn and Miguel to have their turn. While I'm waiting I'll reread the Boys of Brighton series!" —Debbie Kay on *Saint*

"Ms. Tasia has done it again! This is Saint's story, for readers of the Brighton Boys, you'll know he needs a break! After being forced to become a plastic surgeon by his father, he rebels by assisting people in 3rd world countries, which puts him in the position to be kidnapped and tortured. You really feel for him, that's for sure! Max is the perfect man for poor Saint's battered soul, not that he doesn't have his own issues! Overall, this was engaging, steady paced and chock full of all the feels!" —Avid Reader on *Saint*

"Finn and Miguel stole my heart. This is a great Sunday afternoon read. Finn's character jumped off the page as his story developed through each chapter. I loved reading his truth and watching him and Miguel find their home in each other." —K.A. Brown on *Finn*

"Another tale from the Gates of Heaven, another two brilliant MCs we get to know very well. I loved both the plot and the characters, all their emotions and insecurities on full display. All the descriptions and world building were very vivid, providing a great background for an emotional story of self discovery and developing attraction." —AL on *Finn*

"James...what can I say. I couldn't put it down. This is my first book in the series, so it definitely can be read and enjoyed as a standalone, but it will not be my last. Now I'm going to read the previous stories. Solid writing with a gripping style, characters that are right up my alley, and the kind of chemistry I love in my romances. What more do you need for a great reading experience." —cinnamon on *James*

"This is really a great series and I def recommend it. I loved James and Ross, it was a rough start for the two, but they worked it out. I can't wait for more, love everything M. TASIA writes!" — TammyKay on *James*

"I may have my new favorite book couple of the series. Joey and Sam just have that something special. At one point I was ugly crying but it was a good ugly cry if that makes any sense. I really love the series and I can't wait for her next installment!!" —Vine Voice on *Joey*

"M. Tasia is an automatic 1 click author for me...she definitely didn't disappoint with Joey." —Heather Weissman on *Joey*

www.BOROUGHSPUBLISHINGGROUP.com

PUBLISHER'S NOTE: This is a work of fiction. Names, characters, places and incidents either are the product of the author's imagination or are used fictitiously. Any resemblance to actual events, locales, business establishments or persons, living or dead, is coincidental. Boroughs Publishing Group does not have any control over and does not assume responsibility for author or third-party websites, blogs or critiques or their content.

BRADLEY
Copyright © 2020 M. Tasia

ISBN 978-1-951055-79-0

This has been possible because of the love and support of my family.
Love you Craig, Samantha, Katie, and Jason.

ACKNOWLEDGMENTS

Thank you to my amazing publisher for taking the time to play tour guide in her diverse and stunning area of Southern California. Your indomitable spirit and strength inspires me to continue to grow as an author. Also, to my sisters-in-law, thank you for coming along and supporting my dream. The love and strength of family is the cornerstone of my career.

BRADLEY

Chapter One

People stop what they're doing at the sound of breaking glass. Brad felt the weight of everyone's stares as he watched as the Napa Valley red pool onto the tiled floor beneath his feet. The shards from what used to be a fuckin' fancy wine glass sparkled in the noonday sun that streamed through the tall windows of The Gates. That had been the third time today he'd dropped an order, and he could feel his face warming.

He flexed the numb fingers of his left hand into a fist while a rush of anger washed over him. He'd gone straight, in a non-felony kind of way, and was trying to live a "square" life." Regular job, bosses, clocking in, schedules, be nice to the customers, smile—all that shit and more. But his career as a bartender was definitely hanging in the balance. For the four thousandth time, he rethought leaving his life of crime. Yeah, he might be dead by now if he hadn't, but so what?

"Brad, you okay, man?" Finn, his supervisor, asked as he came around the end of the bar, mop in hand.

"I'm sorry," Brad said. "I keep forgetting not to use my left hand. I'll pay for the losses."

The real gut punch: Brad was left-handed.

"Don't worry about it," Finn assured. The boss was a good guy. The owner and management were all good people. That's why Brad hated having to leave, but at this rate, maybe it was for the best before they had no other choice but to fire him.

He reached for the mop, but Finn snatched it away. "I'll get this. Saint and Max want to talk to you in the office."

There it was. Brad had screwed up too many times since coming back after healing from the gunshot wound to his arm months before. He nodded. There was no point in saying anything, and Finn had no control over what Saint would do. What was done was done.

Several patrons gave Brad looks of sympathy, and a few others laughed. Brad had never reveled in someone else's pain. Well, that wasn't entirely true. He loved to see the wealthy criminal element squirm when he relieved them of one item or another. Of course, it hadn't belonged to them in the first place, and he could fence it for cash. Cash was always best. He didn't have the "infrastructure" to hide bars of gold, and he didn't need paintings or statues. That shit wouldn't feed anyone.

"Fuck it," Brad mumbled under his breath. He didn't want to go back to the life, but he was running out of choices. Even with one messed-up arm, he still had more skill than most burglars out there.

He held his head high when he knocked on the office door. He tried not to let shit get to him, and even if this hurt more than usual, he'd carry on.

"Come in," Saint's voice called from behind the closed door.

He didn't hesitate, reaching for the door handle with his left hand before catching himself. With a loud huff, he switched hands, turned the knob, and walked in. Thankfully, it was only Saint and Max in the office. Saint owned The Gates, and Max owned and ran the construction company that was working on the renovation of the old turn-of-the-century building. Along with being Saint's partner in all things, Max was a badass.

"Thank you for coming, Brad," Saint said. "Please have a seat."

Both bosses were sitting behind Saint's large wooden desk, an effective barrier between them and him. Easier to distance oneself from a distasteful situation with a couple of hundred pounds of wood between you and the subject.

Brad didn't sit. "Look, I know you've gotta do whatcha gotta do. It's not personal, it's business. I get it."

Saint and Max looked at each other before turning back to him. "Get what?"

Seriously, they were going to make him say it. "Why you need to fire me." There, now on with it. Maybe he'd still have time to stop by Charlie's on the way to his apartment. Put out a couple of feelers to see who's looking for his services. Even thinking about returning to that life soured his stomach. But what choice did he have?

"Fire you? I didn't call you in here to fire you," Saint stated.

"I've been breaking glasses every day for the past few months," Brad said. "Why wouldn't you fire me?"

"We're not in the habit of firing family," Max grunted. "You were shot protecting Sam and Captain Meyers. You can break as many damn glasses as you want to."

Brad doubted he'd forget the night he almost lost his arm. His co-worker, Joey had a nutso grandfather, a local crime boss, who had kidnapped Joey. Brad used the skills he'd honed as a cat burglar to break into the mansion. Joey was found unhurt. That was all that mattered. The little dude was as sweet as they came, but wasn't what you'd call tough. Brad had gotten shot for his trouble while protecting LAPD captain Eric Meyers. Fucked up his arm and hand, but, hey, life in the fast lane.

"How's your arm?" Saint asked. "Are you in any pain?"

Well, shit. Not fired, and now he had to *share*. "I promise to be more cautious about using my left hand to pick up anything." Brad knew he was avoiding the question, but what good was it to tell them that his arm throbbed so severely he could barely sleep.

"That's not what I asked." Saint sat back, obviously wanting answers.

"It throbs sometimes, but I can handle it, no problem."

"Has your doctor set you up with PT?" Max asked.

Now would not be the best time to let them in on the fact that after being released from the hospital, Brad never returned to see anyone. He took the stitches out himself. Hospitals, follow-up appointments, PT were expensive, and not for the first time, he chastised himself for not putting any real money aside.

"No, I'll be fine without it."

"That what the doctor said?" Saint scowled.

"Um...."

"You didn't go back, did you?" Max leaned forward, but at Saint's touch to his boyfriend's back, Max stopped interrogating.

"We have something for you," Saint said before sliding a folder across the table toward him.

Brad took a seat in one of the two chairs in front of the desk and picked up the folder. The papers inside looked official and had Brad's name all over them. He read the top of the page: "Jacobson Insurance Plan."

"Insurance plan?"

"Yes," Saint answered. "The DTLA community has embraced The Gates, and we have clientele from all over the city who have turned into regulars. As a thank you for everyone's hard work, we're extending our health benefits coverage."

"The plan provides PT for twenty-six visits," Max explained. "You have a doctor's appointment at three this afternoon. She'll give you the script for the PT. It's only a couple blocks over. We'll give you the address."

Brad looked from the pieces of paper in front of him and back to his bosses at least four times before he could get his mouth to work. "Why? What's the catch?" He had to know. People in Brad's life usually looked out for themselves.

Max shook his head. "The catch is, you go to PT, and we get our bartender back at full speed. It costs too much and takes too much damn time to train someone new."

"It's saving us the huge headache and paperwork of a new employee," Saint agreed while looking anywhere but at Brad. The man was a horrible liar. "Now get back out there and take over for Finn. I'll give you the doctor's address and phone number later this afternoon before you leave."

Were these people real?

"Everyone is getting the same benefits, right?" If Brad was the only one, he'd refuse in a heartbeat.

"Yes, everyone," Saint assured. "We need all of you to be healthy as we grow bigger and get busier. Now, go. I have calls to make."

Brad found it hilarious when Saint tried to be tough. The guy was the size of a truck with muscles to spare, but had the softest heart of anyone he'd ever met. It had to be the doctor in him. But anyone looking to take advantage of the boss's nature had to deal with Max. No one in their right mind wanted to take on Max.

"Yeah. Right." He stood. "And…uh, thanks."

As Brad was walking out, he heard Max whisper, "What calls, babe?" Which further confirmed Saint's bravado was all for show.

Brad didn't think people like this existed, or at least not any in his world. He was becoming attached to the crazy crew and could picture staying on long term if his arm healed properly.

He'd find a way to thank them for being so decent.

Chapter Two

Brad cursed the day he'd ever met Saint and took the position as a bartender at The Gates.

"One more time," the sadistic woman cheered. Beads of sweat dripped down Brad's face onto the padded table in front of him. "You can do it. Then we'll take a break."

Grudgingly, using only his left arm and hand, he picked up the one-pound weight and lifted it two inches off the table before rotating his wrist in clockwise circles. His arm was throbbing, but he had to admit whatever his torturer was doing seemed to be working.

He'd been coming to PT twice a week for the last month, and his arm was slowly getting stronger. However, he was paying for every step forward with sweat and pain. This broad, Jo, had given him giant rubber bands to do his "exercises" between visits. Two pages of exercises, if you could believe that shit. She was killing him, and seemed to enjoy every fuckin' minute of it.

"That's it. Five more seconds."

The muscles around the puckered scar on his left bicep refused to loosen and pulled with every move he made. Between the weights, the rubber bands, and the sponge ball, he'd been gaining strength but not mobility. Jo said it would take time, especially since he'd waited so long to start PT. Brad wasn't the patient type, and he sure as shit didn't like to be reminded he could've felt better sooner.

"Okay, good job," Jo praised cheerily. "Take ten minutes to rest and then we'll get back to it."

"Thank god," Brad moaned. "You're evil."

As always, she smiled wide and bounced back into her office as if he'd given her a kick-ass compliment. Weird broad.

He needed some air, and he headed for the door. He wasn't sure how much "fresh air" he'd get in DTLA, but it was better than waiting here for his torture to resume. The breeze was cooler in the evening, and he shivered as it blew through the sweat on his t-shirt.

He leaned against the building's smooth stone, still warm from the afternoon sun.

Music was playing from the gym beside the PT facility, upbeat and fast-paced. He assumed there was some sort of group workout going on when he looked over to see a bunch of people racing each other on stationary bikes. Brad would sooner eat mud then hop onto one of those. The only legitimate reason to peddle that fast was if someone was chasing you.

Given the state of his t-shirt, it looked like he'd cycled for three hours. He was using the front hem to wipe sweat droplets from his hairline when he heard a familiar voice.

"Hello, Bradley."

Ah, shit. Of all the places in the five hundred square miles that made up the city of LA either of them could possibly be, of course, they were on the same six-foot-wide patch of concrete.

"Captain Meyers," Brad said without lowering his shirt until he'd dried his face completely. He knew what he'd see when he did—forbidden fruit. Brad almost made himself laugh, knowing Meyers was the kind of fruit that Brad would likely be deathly allergic to.

He dropped his shirt, and sure enough, the handsome bastard was standing directly in front of him. Meyers's dark eyes seemed to burrow into Brad, making him feel twitchy. The captain was Bigfoot tall with a broad chest Brad wanted to put his hands all over. Meyers wore a t-shirt and a pair of shorts, and was carrying what looked to be a gym bag, confirming that the incredibly attractive police captain worked out right next door to Brad's PT.

Great.

Fate was screwing with him yet again. How could he, of all people, be interested in a cop? Not just any cop—a top cop who acted like captain courageous.

Hell, why would a lawman want to be with a retired burglar?

***

"I've told you repeatedly to call me Eric," Meyers said while his eyes roamed Brad.

His perusal of the man's tight, toned body was unceremoniously interrupted when the object of his fascination lowered his shirt.

"Eric," Brad corrected. "And I'm Brad, not Bradley."

"I like Bradley."

Brad looked uncomfortable and crossed his arms over his toned chest in an attempt to cut off any further conversation, which Eric found interesting. However, now was not the time to do anything but brush the surface, so he examined the healing scar on Brad's upper arm. A stark and permanent reminder that the hardass criminal took a bullet protecting Eric, a cop.

"How's your arm healing?" Eric asked, not expecting a truthful answer.

"Good." By his tone alone, Eric knew Bradley was lying. The pain etched on his face from whatever he'd been doing was plain to see.

Okay, he could work with one-word answers. "Is this where you go to PT?"

"Ah, yeah."

Eric wanted to laugh at the obstinate looks Brad was shooting his way. Wisely, Eric thought the better of it.

"When?" Eric asked quickly. Rapid-fire questions tended to result in the most honest answers instead of allowing Brad time to think up a less than truthful response.

"Right now. Every Tuesday and Thursday at six." His eyebrows scrunched together as he answered, making Eric pause for a fraction of a second to admire the tempting man.

He quickly got himself back under control and asked, "You leave from The Gates or your apartment?"

"Gates."

"Okay. From this point on, I'll be picking you up every Tuesday and Thursday. You can go to PT while I work out." Perfect solution, and then it would give him the ideal opportunity to learn more about this unexpected attraction while helping insure Brad made every PT appointment.

"What?" Brad sputtered.

"After PT, I'll drive you home. You don't need to be walking ten blocks when you're in pain." Eric had beaten himself up for what he'd allowed to happen to Brad, and he never got past feeling like shit that the guy got shot. Gratitude over saving his life was top of his list, but Brad didn't want to hear it, and Eric boxed it away alongside the guilt he carried around every day.

"Sorry? You know where I live?" Brad gave Eric a what-the-fuck look.

"I'll be in the back of The Gates at five-thirty this Thursday," Eric stated. "Don't make me wait. Good night, Bradley."

Eric turned and walked toward the parking garage across the street, leaving Brad growling.

Eric choked back his chuckle and thought, *That went well.*

***

The clock on the wall was drawing closer to five-thirty at lightning speed. Two days ago, stupidly, Brad had stepped outside the PT facility to get a breath of air. Instead, his throat had clogged when Captain Eric Meyers came out of the gym next door.

Was Eric serious with that domineering bullshit? He might be a cop, and he was taller than Brad, but Brad was nobody's bitch. On the other hand, Meyers was shit-hot, and Brad wouldn't mind getting a piece of that.

His head hurt from the back and forth, and his constant indecision about meeting Eric out back—there was no reason Brad couldn't go out the front door and hightail it to PT—had been fucking with his head all day. Two broken tumblers and a Bloody Mary made with peach schnapps instead of vodka added to the list of fuckups for the day.

The customer had sprayed a mouthful of the liquid clear across two tables after taking a big gulp of what had to be a heinous drink. Thankfully, Finn came out and calmed the guy down before the customer dove over the bar at Brad, thinking that he'd been punk'd or something. A few comped meals nullified his rage enough for Brad to continue with his day, though he made sure to move the schnapps out of reach.

"So, wanna tell me what's got your boxers in a bunch?" Joey asked as he rounded the end of the bar.

Brad wasn't sure how to answer, so he went with denial. "I'm good."

"Yeah, let's try this again," Joey said. "You nervous because Captain Meyers is on his way to pick you up?"

Brad spun around to face Joey. "How'd you know?" It wasn't as if Brad had told anyone.

His friend smiled wide. "You do remember my boyfriend, Sam, is a cop, right?"

"Eric's been telling everyone he's picking me up for my PT appointment?" Why would he do that?

"Eric?" Joey's eyebrows shot up his forehead as he chuckled.

Shit.

"He told me to call him that." That explanation sounded pathetic.

"Hmm. Every time I've talked to him, I've used Captain Meyers, and he's never corrected me." Those eyebrows of his were now wiggling suggestively.

"It doesn't matter," Brad said. "I've decided I'm going to walk." He didn't need this shit.

Joey's face changed from amused to concerned. "Why? Is something wrong? Was he mean to you? What did he say?"

Leave it to the kind-hearted guy to worry about Brad's feelings. "No, he was fine. Pushy, but fine."

Joey's amused expression returned. "So, what's wrong with accepting a ride from him?"

Because he's a cop, he's domineering, he's a cop, he's overwhelming, he confuses me, and it's worth repeating, he's a cop. All valid answers, but Brad went with the basics. "Nothing, I guess."

"Good, because he's waiting out back for you right now," Joey said before shoving his cellphone back into his pocket.

"Damn it."

"Off you go. PT awaits," Joey poked while pushing Brad away from the bar. "Go, get better."

Brad grabbed his backpack from one of the cupboards and had no other choice but to head for the back door. Fine, of course he had the choice, but nothing as appealing as what was waiting for him out back.

Admit it. You want to see the cop again. Brad was going to strangle that little voice in the back of his head one of these days. That voice had stuck around longer than his parents had. Grandma Carol would tell him it was his conscience trying to reason with him. Brad didn't care what it was. He wished it would shut the fuck up.

He weaved through the tall storage racks in the back of the restaurant until he came to the big-ass steel door and touchpad guarding the rear entrance to the building. Brad had to admit he was itching to peek inside the security system that friends of Saint's, one of the Sentinels, installed and have a look around. Not to steal anything, but for the thrill of being able to take it apart without anyone being the wiser.

Brad had always been interested in puzzles as a child. The harder they were, the happier he was. Burglarizing known criminals' homes had begun as a bit of a test, where he was never really taking anything of value. Disarming their security systems were merely another puzzle that, as it turned out, he was exceptionally good at decoding. He often compared it to having blueprints in his mind. Later on, this ability became a necessary means to an end.

Taking a deep breath, he placed his palm on the pad and watched as the green bar of light ghosted over his hand. He'd only been given access a few weeks ago, proving that perhaps the bosses were beginning to trust him after all. They were big on safety and security around here. Learning that Saint had been kidnapped and tortured while on a medical aid mission in some jungle made Brad understand why Saint was extra cautious.

The scrape of metal bolts sliding back from the door echoed through the storage room, and Brad reached for the handle. Sunlight poured in the moment he cracked the metal behemoth open. Initially, he'd been shocked by how easily the door maneuvered for such a large piece of steel. These Sentinels knew what they were doing.

Once his eyes adjusted to the sunlight, Brad saw Eric's truck among the other vehicles parked in the private lot behind The Gates. It wasn't the latest model or covered in shiny chrome, but it was clean and well taken care of. Big and intimidating like its owner.

Brad was careful to shut the door and wait to hear the bolts slide back into place before descending the metal stairs and walking to the truck. When he neared it, Eric stepped out from the driver's side and rounded the front to open the passenger door for Brad.

The move confused him. He wasn't an invalid, and he sure as fuck wasn't dating the guy, but he went with the flow and stepped around Eric, who was still in uniform, and took a seat inside.

"Thank you," Brad grumbled.

"You're welcome, Bradley," Eric said in that deep, growly voice that drove Brad crazy. "Buckle up."

When he reached for his seatbelt, he'd been so distracted by the big guy that Brad used his left hand. He hissed in pain and immediately pulled his arm back against his chest. He twisted and reached with his right hand to grab the belt when Eric's body eclipsed the sunlight beating into the cab.

That wide chest was only inches from Brad's face, and the smell of Eric's earthy, smoky cologne filled his senses. He felt suspended in that moment, the warmth of the captain's tanned skin so close he could feel it, right up until he heard the click.

Brad leaned back as far as he could and tried to calm what had to be his flushed face. Leave it to him to want to soak in the guy's scent when the dude was simply helping Brad with his seatbelt. Yep, a highlight of the evening this was not, and one hell of a way to start whatever this arrangement was.

When Eric pulled away, those dark eyes penetrated straight through Brad. "Are you in a lot of pain?"

Hmmm, the truth sucked, but by the look on Eric's face, that's what he expected. "It varies on the day depending on how busy The Gates gets and how many times I screw up."

"And today?"

"Was a busy day."

"Understood," Eric said before stepping back and closing the truck door.

Brad couldn't help but admire the way Eric's navy-blue uniform molded to his body. Wasn't there some sort of rule about cops looking shit-hot sexy while working? There should be, because damn, he was distracting.

Brad shook his head and forced himself to look out the side window at the parking garage across the street. That's where most employees and guests at The Gates parked, and once the remaining condos were complete, where the owners would park as well. Only the people living in the hub parked in the private lot out back. Saint, Max, Marian—if she had a car. Since Joey and Sam had purchased the first completed unit after the sale of Sam's old family condo, they'd begun parking across the street.

Eric opened the driver's door and hopped in behind the wheel. The truck rumbled to life, and without another word, he pulled in front of the gate, glaring out the windshield, waiting until the sensor signaled the solid metal to roll. Then, his jaw muscle jumping, he accelerated onto the street and headed in the direction of the gym and PT.

Brad couldn't help but feel as though he'd done something wrong. It was strange and unsettling, and he didn't like it much. "Did I say or do something to tick you off, man?"

The captain seemed to come out of whatever trance was causing him to grind his teeth, and glanced over at him.

"No, of course not." The big guy looked honestly confused by the question.

"Then mind explaining why you look ready to strangle your steering wheel?"

Eric loosened his grip and stretched out his fingers. "Sorry."

Brad decided it was best to let it go. Hell, maybe the guy had anger issues. Lots of cops seemed pissed off all the time. And really, what did Brad know about the captain? The drive didn't take long, and soon, Eric was parking in the reserved spots on the other side of the street from the gym. Brad got out and grabbed his backpack off the seat before closing the door.

Eric placed his hand at the small of Brad's back and led him across the four-lane street. When they reached the other side, he veered away and headed toward the PT facility. For some reason, Eric followed and walked him to the door.

"I'm okay from here on," Brad said. Eric looked like he wanted to say something, and Brad knew he should've gone out the front door of The Gates and walked his ass over here. "What?"

"I want to make it clear. I wasn't angry with you." Eric's hands waved in the air as he talked. Brad had noticed these gestures before, but the movement seemed more pronounced now.

"Then, who?" Cause sure as shit he'd been the only other person in the truck.

"Myself," Eric admitted. "You should have never been put in a dangerous situation. Now you're suffering because of my inability to keep you safe. So, yeah, I'm pissed at myself for allowing that to happen." Before Brad had a chance to respond, Eric continued. "Wait for me here if I'm late, and I'll drive you home." Then he turned and walked over to the front doors of the gym and disappeared inside.

Brad stood glued to the spot on the sidewalk, trying to make sense of what he'd heard.

He blames himself for my gunshot wound.

Brad could feel the anxiety melt out of his body. The only reason Captain Meyers wanted anything to do with him was out of guilt. That's all this was about in the end. There wasn't any other reason.

As the truth sank in, Brad realized that maybe, in some way, he was disappointed. Which didn't make sense. Yeah, the guy was hot, but so were about five hundred thousand other dudes in LA. If Brad wanted to get him some, there was plenty of talent to choose from. No way was he interested in getting anything started with a cop.

Chapter Three

"That you?" Grandma Carol yelled from the living room as Brad walked into their two-bedroom apartment.

"Yeah," he replied. "How many other people have keys to the front door?"

"Don't get smart with me, young man. I can still turn you over my knee."

Brad couldn't help but laugh while making his way to the well-loved living room. Crocheted white doilies graced every available flat surface, faded landscapes hung on the walls, and a large plastic-covered flowered couch sat against the far wall, hermetically sealed and only used by guests.

"You haven't been able to do that in years. Remember, you almost threw your back out trying to lift me when I was eleven. I think that's about the same time you began chasing me around with a wooden spoon instead."

"You were a hellion. There was no stopping you," she grumbled.

"Lies, lies. I was an angel. All the neighbors were jealous of you for how well I behaved." Even he couldn't keep a straight face saying those words.

"Behaved, my ass. The neighbors couldn't understand why I didn't toss you out on your ear." She puffed up, sitting a bit straighter. He loved riling his Grams up. "I seriously considered sending you to that home for wayward boys."

"Wayward? You love me, and I know it, so stop trying to act tough, old lady," Brad teased.

"Years of my life raising you, and what do I get for it, this?" She waved her arthritic hand up and down in front of him.

"Yeah, yeah, yeah. Horrible child. Good for nothing." He chuckled and bent to kiss the top of her grey head. "How was your day, Grams?"

"Good, sweetheart," she said before hugging him. "Mrs. Jesvic from five-B came by today for a visit. That granddaughter of hers needs a steady boyfriend. She stays out all these late hours, and it's scaring Mrs. Jesvic half to death."

His grandmother looked at him the way she did whenever she wanted something. "No, Grams. Not a chance. Whatever you got brewing in that head of yours, forget it. I prefer my dates to be of the male variety."

"Fine, then bring a nice boy home to meet me," she groused. "Hell, I would take even a friend. You never have anyone but me."

Brad couldn't help himself and began to sing. "There's only you in my life…"

"Don't sing old Lionel Richie songs to me, mister. I'm serious."

"Would you prefer a little rap instead?"

She leaned back in her fancy Louis XV Bergere chair and stared him down. Grandma had taken one look at it in the photos he used to case a joint and claimed it for her own. Brad was almost sure Mr. Verchenko had forgotten about it by now. Brad figured the guy would have been more concerned over the ten flawless diamonds he'd "repatriated" from the small steel safe that sat hidden behind a collection of poetry and one of Shakespeare's "First Folios." Too bad Brad wasn't into rare books, or that would have been one hell of a score.

Alas, books were harder to fence, so he stayed in his lane. Jewelry, coins, and such all used to be his stock and trade. That damn chair of hers nearly got him caught, but after seeing her get years of enjoyment out of it, he could look past the hours it took for him to trudge it home without anyone seeing him.

"How was work?" she asked.

"Fine. Almost poisoned a man." Brad slowly removed his jacket to avoid jarring his aching arm.

"Poisoned?" Grams thin eyebrows shot up.

"Nothing a few free meals couldn't fix." He waved her concern off.

"Okay," she said while turning her shrewd eyes on him. "How was PT?"

"Painful, but again, fine," Brad answered with a huff. "Why don't we skip ahead and get to the question you want to ask me?"

"All right." She grinned evilly. "How was your time with the captain?"

If she wasn't fixing up the neighbors, his grandma never missed an opportunity to find him a match. "I arrived safely at my appointment, and obviously home as well."

"That's it?" she asked in a slightly shrill tone. "Isn't he the one that you have the hots for?"

"The hots, Grams? Seriously?" Brad brushed a stray curl away from in front of his eyes. He needed a haircut. What man in their right mind wanted curls in his eyes? He tried to keep it short most of the time, but couldn't buzz it himself since his dominant hand didn't work. He hated the idea of going to a stylist. There were a few old-school barbers around. He'd have to hit one of them to tame the mess.

"I saw that look when you talked about that captain fellow. You can't fool this old woman. I know you're interested in him." She looked offended that he'd question her intuition.

"Even if I was, he's a cop, remember? The exact opposite of what I am, a burglar. Plain and simple, Grams."

"So, it's like that is it? Black and white, no grey."

"How 'bout right and wrong, cops and robbers, Grams."

"You're not a burglar anymore," she said with conviction, as if that one fact changed a lifetime of criminal behavior.

"That doesn't erase what I've done," Brad explained. "No, I don't think my former profession bodes well for a future with the police captain. Besides, he told me tonight that he felt sorry for me because I got hurt on his watch or some shit like that. All he feels is guilt."

"You didn't have a choice back then."

"Yes, I did. I can't magically forget what I've done, and FYI, I'd probably do it all over again." Facts were facts. His Grams was a hopeless romantic, married to the same man for over fifty years before Gramps passed on.

"I don't know about that, but I'll leave it be if that's what you want."

"Yeah. That's what I want. Please." He knew this wouldn't be the last time he heard about this.

"Okay, consider it shelved," she agreed. "For now."

"Grams…"

"Fine. Did you make that stop for me on your way home?" Her face lit up so fast that he couldn't help but smile.

"Of course I did. Would I ever forget something this important?"

Eric had taken him after PT. The funny thing was, the captain hadn't even asked what Brad was picking up. He'd imagined being a cop would have made him a bit curious, but there was not even a second glance when he'd asked to stop.

Remember, it's guilt that's making him do this. He's not interested in any other part of my life. Keep that straight.

"And...?"

Brad laughed as he reached for his backpack. "You know you're addicted to this shit. I don't want to be your dealer."

"Shut up and hand them over."

He shook his head and pulled out a small paper bag. "Here."

She snatched the bag out of his hands and peeked inside. A satisfied smile crossed her lips as she took stock of her new stash. "Three scratcher tickets and a bag of black licorice. You're the best grandson."

"I'm your only grandson," he corrected.

"Technicalities. Dinner's in the oven. You can reheat it in the microwave if you want. I made your favorite," Grams muttered. She was already searching for something to use to scratch off her tickets.

"Cabbage rolls?" Things were looking up.

"Go see for yourself and let me alone," she said while picking up a loose quarter from her side table. "I've got some scratchin' to do."

Brad retreated into the kitchen and pulled a casserole dish from the oven before flipping back the tin foil to reveal the cabbage-wrapped goodness. He didn't know what he'd do without his Grams.

He would, and had, gone to any lengths to keep her healthy and safe.

***

On his way to the bathroom for a much-needed shower, Eric threw his gym bag onto the bench at the foot of his bed. Usually, he took a shower at the gym after his workout, but today he didn't want to be late in case Brad was waiting for him outside.

What was wrong with him? Eric didn't change his routine for anybody. Of course, he felt sorry for the guy. Brad had risked his life to help save a friend. Then went as far as taking a bullet meant for Eric. Even after admitting he was a retired burglar to a room full of cops, Brad didn't back down.

Without him and his ability to break into about anywhere, they would have been in more danger rushing into the house. Brad had never blamed anyone on the team for his injury. He simply accepted it as part of what he had to do to save Joey, and carried on.

Eric had to admit, the man intrigued him, but being attracted to him was a bit harder to accept. He knew better and had learned his lesson. He couldn't let that shit happen again. No matter how much he wanted to run his fingers through the handsome man's curly blond hair or stare into those hypnotic hazel eyes.

Damnit.

That shit was off-limits. Period.

Eric's cellphone rang just as he was about to strip out of his damp t-shirt and shorts. Of course, he picked it up. He was on the job 24/7.

"Captain Meyers."

"Son, good to hear your voice. That you're alive. I thought you'd fallen off the face of the earth." His mother's loud voice had him pulling the phone a few inches away from his ear.

"Hello, Mom." Eric couldn't help but laugh. "I'm fine. It's been a little busy around the station recently."

"You work too hard. You need a break," she scolded. He could hear the question on the tip of her tongue before another word was uttered. "Why don't you come down for a visit?"

"Mom, sneaking away to Florida isn't in my schedule until Christmas. You know that."

"Can't a mom miss her only child?"

"Oh god, Mom. Don't start." She had the knack for making him feel like he was sixteen again.

Her tinkling laughter had him shaking his head. She was the best, the absolute best, and he loved her more than anything. "I know, honey. You make me proud by how hard you work, keeping people in LA safe. Maybe we'll come out to visit you."

"You know I have an extra bedroom, and you're always welcome here. Let me know when you're thinking, and I'll clean up the spare room and put new sheets out."

"That'd be wonderful, dear," his mom said.

"How are you feeling?" His amazing mother had been fighting high blood pressure for years. She was currently on three different medications to keep it under control. High blood pressure caused her to suffer from seriously bad headaches and chest pains, which scared the shit out of him.

"Oh, don't you worry. Dr. Anderson is taking outstanding care of me," she said. "Oh, hold on, honey, Dan wants to speak with you. I'll see you soon. Love you."

"Love you too, Mom," Eric said and then waited for his stepdad to get on the line. The only thing the two of them could agree on was the need for his mom to be taken care of, and Dan seemed to do an excellent job of it, according to his mom.

"Yeah, Eric, how's the station house?" Dan asked, not shocking Eric in the least. Being a former police captain himself, Dan was more interested in the workings of the LAPD than his stepson's life. The days of Eric caring what the man thought were long over.

"Same as every other day—busy."

"Yeah, criminals don't take holidays," he grumbled and then coughed right into the receiver. *Nice.* "You're right to not come for a visit."

If for no other reason, than I don't' want to see you.

Eric would love to get his mom to himself so they could talk without Dan hovering.

"What? I didn't hear you."

Shit. Had he said that out loud? "I said, I know that."

"Good. You stay there and do your job," he ordered as if Eric needed to be scolded or something. Christ, this guy was a piece of work.

Eric ignored his stepfather as he'd been doing for years. The man couldn't help question him about his ability to be captain, if he was working hard enough, that he had the family's valuable reputation to keep, and more shit along those lines.

Time for a change of subject. "How did mom make out with the cardiologist?"

"We didn't go."

"What? Why?" They'd all been waiting over ten months for her to get into see this specialist. She came highly recommended.

"It was raining that day," he said. "You know I don't drive in the rain."

Eric could feel his blood pressure rising. "Why didn't you call a taxi or Lyft?"

"Taxi? That costs an arm and a leg. We're on a tight budget with only our pensions to live off. Can't spend money needlessly." He talked like her heart wasn't a priority.

"You have a good pension, you don't have a mortgage because I paid it off, and I send you money every two weeks. Hell, I would have transferred the money to you if you needed it for the taxi. Mom needed that appointment."

"Don't you get mouthy with me, boy. I'm all Janet has, and I do the best I can."

Lies slithered into Eric's ear, but he fought not to explode. The fuckin' greedy bastard. Yeah, Dan did the best he could because Eric was paying all the bills. Of course, his mom didn't know that. He'd do anything to ensure her blood pressure wouldn't get worse.

They'd had this conversation too many times to count. "Did you at least reschedule the appointment?"

"I'm not stupid. I was running a station full of officers when you were still shitting in your diapers."

Eric didn't even bother acknowledging his comment. "When is it?"

"November twelfth at one."

"How is she feeling?" He had asked his mom, but she didn't tell him the whole truth. She didn't want to worry him.

"Her blood pressure is still high. It's best to keep things calm for her." Like clockwork, Dan segued onto his favorite tortured topic. "You keep your dick in your pants? Your mom doesn't need to hear about you getting off with other men. With her blood pressure, it'll kill her for sure."

Eric regretted the day he'd come out at fifteen to his stepdad and every day since. The bastard was as homophobic as they came. He didn't know how his mother would feel about him being gay. He wasn't afraid to tell her, but he didn't want the never-ending bullshit Dan would dredge up to affect Mom's health. No shit, if he could find a way to get the guy gone, Eric would do it.

"If you even think it's going to rain on November twelfth, you let me know, and I'll arrange a car service. Don't you dare cancel another appointment," Eric growled as he hit the end button a bit harder than he'd intended. A spiderweb of cracks spread across the bottom half of his screen, and he set down the phone on the edge of the bathroom sink before breaking it further.

He looked at his reflection in the mirror and despised the man looking back at him. Weak. No matter how hard he worked out or how well he led his officers, the fact remained that he was weak.

All thoughts of the intriguing man he'd been slowly trying to get closer to were now tainted by his stepdad's words. Brad's unsure smile and ever-watchful eyes seemed to fade into the background as Eric's reality came into sharp focus.

If only his mother weren't so happy with Dan, Eric would scoop her up from Florida and bring her back to LA in a heartbeat. However, any time she talked about her life in Florida, she always sounded so happy, and he couldn't bring himself to ruin that for her.

Keep it in your pants. The words floated around in Eric's head. Damn, he'd been cautious, picking guys up online, no commitment, no history, no emotions. To be honest, he was more intimate with his right hand than any human, and he was tired of it. Lonely night after lonely night. They began to add up, and he yearned for something more than the odd hookup.

He was desperate to hold onto the feeling he had when Bradley had been so close to him, but it was compromised by the layers of shit in Eric's life. Eventually, he gave up altogether. Though he swore he would help in any way to insure the man healed properly, it was becoming obvious nothing more could come of it. He wanted to kick himself for even toying with the idea of getting close to Bradley.

His mom had worked hard to raise Eric on her own before Dan showed up, and she never complained about it. Keeping her happy was his job. Janet Meyers-Smith was an angel, and Eric would do anything to guarantee she had the best for the rest of her life.

If that meant no comfort in this life, then he could live with that.

Right now, there was no other choice.

Chapter Four

Brad watched Eric out of the corner of his eye. Something was wrong with the captain, but Brad couldn't figure out what. As he had been every Tuesday and Thursday, Eric was waiting out back behind The Gates, but it felt different. After the first time they'd ridden together, Eric had become more withdrawn, and while Brad didn't mind the quiet, it seemed there was more to this than a busy man mulling over his day.

They'd established a routine of sorts over the past couple of weeks. Brad would come out the back door, Eric would open the truck's passenger door for him and then buckled him in before driving to the PT facility, parking, and going to the gym. The process repeated itself afterward with the door and buckling, and then Eric drove Brad home, but not before stopping at the convenience store for Grams's ticket and licorice fix.

Brad had slowly become more comfortable with the big guy, and they'd even shared a conversation or two. That few minutes of idle chatter didn't give Brad the right to pry into the captain's private life, even though his sullen expression suggested all was not right in the cop's world. For all he knew, Eric had fought with his girlfriend or boyfriend. *Shit, maybe he's married.* Not everyone wore a ring.

Suddenly, Brad wasn't so curious to learn the truth.

They pulled up outside the convenience store closest to his and Grams's apartment, and Eric threw the truck into park and shut it off.

Without looking over at Brad, he asked. "What?"

"What, what?"

"Seriously, you've been staring at me since the moment we left your appointment, that's what."

"Fine, I was wondering what was bothering you, and if I could help." *Please don't say you and the Mrs. fought.* How would Brad know? They'd never talked about anything other than superficial shit.

When Eric didn't answer, Brad thought maybe sharing something personal about himself might help get the ball rolling. "Do you know why I ask you to stop here every night you drive me home?"

Eric finally looked over at him. "No. It's none of my business."

Though that stung a little, Brad continued. "I live with my Grams, and she and my Gramps had a tradition for many years. Every night they'd scratch their lottery tickets, and Gramps would eat five pieces of black licorice. Only five, never more. He used to say he wasn't a greedy man." Brad waited a moment to see if Eric would say anything. Nada. So Brad continued. "After he passed, I thought it would be a good way to keep his memory going, so every night, I stop on my way home and pick up tickets and licorice for her to have before bed."

Brad hadn't realized how much that memory meant to him until his voice wavered slightly with the last few words. He missed his Gramps.

"You're close with your grandparents?" Eric asked.

"They raised me, and made sure I kept myself off the streets." Without them, he'd have been dead long ago.

"I'm not sure how far 'professional burglar' is from life on the streets," Eric said with a slight laugh and smile. "You're lucky to have had them."

"Don't I know it," Brad agreed. "I'd do and have done anything for them."

The captain gave Brad an assessing look but said nothing more. When the silence continued, Brad became frustrated. "Yo. What gives, man? This is where you tell me what's bothering you. You know, tit for tat, quid pro quo, give and take. You don't seem to have this questioning stuff down. You sure you're a cop?"

Eric smiled again, and it was one of his genuine ones. Brad had seen the captain give his standard smile, being social and polite and stuff. If Brad hadn't seen the real thing, he wouldn't have known what he was missing. He liked this version much better.

"I see," Eric said after a few moments.

He hadn't intended to put the guy on the spot. "It's cool. You don't feel like talking, whatever."

The big guy shifted his body behind the steering wheel and looked at Brad dead on. "How about this? We get to know each other a bit more before I spill my guts."

With a shrug, Brad answered, "Yeah. All right."

"Good," Eric said before taking a breath. "My father passed away when I was five years old. He'd been in the wrong place at the wrong time and interrupted an armed robbery on his way home from work. He'd stopped to get my mother flowers the same as he did every payday and ended up shot after only taking a few steps into the shop."

"Shit, I'm sorry, man." Brad hadn't intended to rip open any wounds. "I shouldn't have guilted that out of you."

Eric's dark brows furrowed. "You didn't, and it was a long time ago. My mother remarried when I was twelve, and as far as I know, she's happy and living in Florida with her husband."

Brad didn't miss the change in Eric's tone when he mentioned his stepfather, but he let it go. Instead, he leaned back against the passenger door to face the captain.

"My mother and father took off before they could even be bothered to give me a first name. Grams named me after her father. She and Gramps took me home from the hospital when I was two days old. I've never met my biologicals to this day."

Eric nodded his head and appeared to be listening intently. Other than his grandparents, Brad couldn't remember anyone paying this close attention to him. Mind, he hadn't been living the kind of life where "sharing" was a thing.

"Their loss," Eric said firmly. "Even if they'd stuck around, I doubt they were parental material. Maybe you were better off with your grandparents."

"Yeah. I've come to the same conclusion. However, I still became a burglar, so maybe I inherited my parents' irresponsibility." Brad could feel the weight of Eric's stare, but refused to look away.

"What made you decide on that type of life? From what I can see, you haven't benefitted from it, or you wouldn't be working as a bartender and living in a rent-controlled building."

Brad wasn't offended by the question. Hell, it was the truth. He and Grams weren't exactly living the high life, but they got by. He preferred ginger ale to champagne anyway.

"I don't think we've gotten to know each other nearly well enough for me to lay that shit out."

Eric bowed his head. "Fair enough."

"Yeah. Who knows, maybe I'll say something the same day you tell me what has you so worried."

"Deal."

Brad turned and opened his door, flooding the cab of the truck with light. "I won't be long." The benefit of doing this run for Grams every night was he already knew the guy who owned the corner store, and he always had the items ready for him to pick up.

The owner, Ted, had been friends with Gramps for as long as Brad could remember. As a child, he'd spent a lot of time here while the two men gossiped about the goings-on in the neighborhood.

Brad walked the last few yards to the open doorway set in the corner of the building. Bright light filtered past the old metal Coke sign and out onto the dark sidewalk as a flashing red oval declared the store OPEN. The warm light had always been welcoming, but as he took his first step into the small store, he knew something was off.

A younger man stood at the front counter across from Ted. Among the colorful branded DTLA knick-knacks, COOLA sunscreen, Abba-Zaba taffy bars, and various candies, Ted's pale face stood as a stark contrast, and even before the stranger turned around Brad knew in his gut he'd walked in on an armed robbery.

Shit.

***

Eric had been fighting his attraction to Bradley for weeks, and his resolve to keep his distance and his fucked-up life to himself was wearing thin. The more he learned about the guy, the more he wanted to know. The man was a walking contradiction. A skilled burglar, which he'd seen in action, wore beat-up Nike's, lived with his grandmother in an old apartment building, and dutifully stopped every night to pick up his Grams's lottery tickets and candy.

Even if he tried, Eric couldn't make that shit up. There was so much more to Bradley than met the eye, and Eric decided to uncover all of it.

He allowed himself to imagine getting closer to Bradley. Fuck what Dan said about Eric being gay. His mother and that POS lived three thousand miles away. She didn't have to know the first thing about his private life. Though the thought of hiding something so fundamentally part of who he was hurt, but Eric would never do anything to upset her, especially given her precarious health. It sucked, and he felt like a pimple-faced teenager all over again fighting for his identity.

Eric didn't know how long he'd sat there ruminating, but he realized Brad was taking much longer than he usually did. His instincts told him brushing off the delay as nothing more than jaw-jackin' with the old man behind the counter would be a mistake. Brad had always gotten his stuff, and came right out.

Eric took his keys out of the ignition and unlocked his reinforced glove box where he kept his police-issued Beretta along with two clips and his badge when he went into the gym. He clipped his badge to the collar of his shirt and loaded one of the clips into the gun. Brad was going to kick his ass if Eric scared the hell out of the old guy, but Eric couldn't fight the voice inside his head telling him that something was wrong.

Quickly he jumped out of his truck, careful not to slam the door to alert anyone to his presence. The street was empty, which was a good thing. Last thing he needed was collateral damage if shit was about to go down. He made his way to the open doorway, calling on all his training and quickly took a look inside before flattening his back against the brick wall once again before taking a few steps back.

Shit. He'd been right. A lone assailant was holding Brad and the old guy at gunpoint. Irony or cosmic fuckery that not ten minutes ago he'd told the story of his father's untimely demise in an armed robbery.

Eric pulled out his phone, turned it to silent, and then texted one of his officers, Sam Weber, with the details of the ongoing situation. Sam would call dispatch and come with backup.

Eric inched back toward the open doorway and concentrated on the voices coming from inside the store. The anger and confusion in the armed man's voice guaranteed there was no chance Eric would be able to wait for the backup to arrive before making a move. The guy sounded strung out, and if that were the case, it wouldn't take much to send him over the edge.

Eric had sworn to himself that nothing was going to happen to Brad ever again on his watch.

Eric intended to keep that oath.

***

Brad watched the rusted barrel of the junkie's gun shake violently in his filthy hand. His arm was a roadmap of drug use and abuse, clear to see as it was snaked around Brad's chest from behind. The junkie's grip was nearly strangling Brad as the pressure increased around his throat. That shit was going to leave marks.

Ted appeared frozen to his spot behind the counter, his arms raised high. Brad's injured arm was taking a beating as he was dragged back and forth in front of a table of Ghirardelli chocolate bars while the junkie paced and shouted.

"Give me the fuckin' money," he yelled in a voice that sounded like he'd smoked a carton of cigarettes before eating the filters.

Ted didn't move. *Shit.* The old guy looked ready to pass out as his face went even paler, and beads of sweat rolled down his typically rosy cheeks. Brad was getting more pissed by the second. Ted didn't deserve this shit.

"Leave him alone," Brad said to the junkie. "I can reach around the counter and open the register."

The pressure around his throat increased until Brad could hear the blood pulsing through his head. His vision began to darken around the edges, and he knew he was close to passing out. If he did, he wouldn't be able to protect Ted.

He gave it another shot. In a strained voice, he said, "I'll get all the money, put it in a bag…along with cigarettes…whatever you want." His head was pounding, and his vision was failing.

The pressure eased slightly. "Try anything, and I'll kill the old man." With that, the junkie released Brad and pointed the gun straight at Ted's head. "Move it."

Brad didn't waste any time and hopped up onto the counter, leaned over, and pushed a few buttons on the cash register. With a ding, the drawer opened. The sight of the small stack of bills caught the man's attention, giving Brad the chance to glance at the front door.

He didn't know whether to be relieved or horrified to find Eric slipping inside the store and down one of the back aisles. Of course, he was aware the captain had been waiting for him outside, but for some reason, he hadn't thought of it until he saw him.

Brad was now worried about *two* people he cared about getting hurt. Hell of a time to realize he cared for the captain more than he'd thought.

"Hurry up," the junkie yelled, waving his gun inches from Ted's face.

Brad slowly reached back to grab a bag off the hook when he saw the Billy club. Its chipped black paint made him wonder how many times Ted had used it before. He lifted an empty plastic bag onto the counter and began stuffing money and cigarettes into it.

As he kept packing, the robber's smile began to grow, featuring his four dark yellow top teeth. Brad chanced a look at the security mirror installed in the corner of the store, which allowed Ted to keep an eye on the coolers in the back. Eric had moved closer, amazing Brad that a man of his size didn't make a sound.

When Brad reached back for a second bag, he took advantage of the junkie's temporary distraction and moved the club closer, but still out of sight. The entire time Ted remained motionless, barely breathing. That bottle of Scotch Ted kept underneath the counter would need to be cracked open once this was over.

Brad continued to stuff more and more cigarettes into the second bag. The longer it took to fill, the more time Eric had to make his move.

"There's a couple packages of lottery tickets back here. You want them?"

Say yes. Say yes.

The junkie's red-rimmed eyes seemed to shine a brighter. "Yeah, throw them bastards in there, but don't try anything or I'll put a hole in the middle," the junkie waved the gun at Ted, "of his forehead."

Brad raised his hands in surrender. "Be cool, man. You're in complete control here." Might as well lay on a heap of flattery to insure the junkie didn't get twitchier than he was already.

The junkie seemed to think it over for a minute before smiling. "Damn right, I'm in charge. Now get me those tickets." Brad lowered his hands and slowly brought his legs up over the counter. "What are you doing?"

"The tickets are on the lowest shelf. I have to go down behind the counter to get them." When the junkie looked like he was about to waver, Brad added, "There's a bank deposit bag down there as well. Should I check it for more money?" There was no bag. But one thing Brad knew from his former life, greed was a powerful master.

"Hurry up, then."

Thankfully, the man's drug-addled brain was more focused on the money, and he hadn't realized he'd lowered the gun he'd been pointing at Ted. He had it lying on the counter in his limp hand as he tried to see what Brad was doing.

Brad jumped down onto the other side of the counter, and with his hands raised, he lowered himself behind it. Instead of reaching for the tickets, he took hold of the Billy club.

"Police, drop your weapon," Eric's voice boomed through the store.

In one fluid motion, Brad pulled Ted down behind the counter and out of harm's way while standing gripping the club in his right hand and bringing it down on the junkie's wrist, making him lose his grip on the gun. Before he could reach for the weapon, Eric rushed forward and tackled the junkie to the ground.

Brad jumped up and over the counter, his heart in his throat, watching the two men wrestle. The junkie fought like a wild animal, but it was only a matter of seconds before the captain had him pinned, face-first against the stained tiled floor.

The store erupted and was suddenly swarming with cops. Brad saw Sam, Joey's man, among the fray before Brad quickly jumped back behind the counter to check on Ted, who was still sitting on the floor next to those lottery tickets.

"Are you okay?" Brad asked while crouching down in front of the older man. "Are you hurt?"

Ted's faded blue eyes regarded Brad as if he wasn't fully aware of his surroundings. "Brad, son. You here for your grandmother's bag?"

Shit. All this shit had to've rattled the old man's cage. He popped his head over the counter and yelled, "We're going to need paramedics," then he went back to concentrating on Ted. "Yes,

Grams loves the licorice and always says that your scratcher tickets are the luckiest."

Behind him, he could hear heavy steps heading straight for him. Brad was unceremoniously lifted into the air and gently set onto the counter. The look on Eric's face surprised him. Fear.

"Where are you hurt?" Eric asked as he lifted Brad's arms and looked under his shirt for wounds. "How bad is it?" He tilted Brad's chin and growled. "Is it your throat? There are bruises around it. Are you having difficulty breathing or swallowing?"

Something warm spread through Brad and settled in his chest. "No, I'm okay. It's Ted. I think he's in shock."

Eric's shoulders lowered as he let out a deep breath. "Okay. Help's on the way." He jumped over the counter like an Olympic gymnast, then knelt beside Ted and offered him his hand. "Would you like to stand, sir?"

"Yes. I'm not sure why I'm on the floor in the first place." Ted took hold of the captain's hand and slowly stood with Eric's help.

"Sam, can you bring over a chair and set it in front here?" Brad asked from his perch on top of the counter as Eric led Ted around to the front of the store.

Brad jumped down and joined Eric, taking Ted's free hand. "It's going to be all right, Ted, but you need to go to the hospital to get checked out."

"Why?" Ted asked.

"You were held up by gunpoint."

"Gunpoint. I think I'd remember that, young man." Ted had called him "young man" from the first day his Gramps had brought him into the store.

They sat Ted down on the chair, and all three watched as officers walked the cuffed robber from the store. "That's okay if you don't remember. We'll get you to the hospital to have you checked out to be safe."

Ted seemed to think about it for a moment. "Are you coming with me?"

"Of course," Brad assured. "I won't leave you. Is there anyone you want us to call?"

"My daughter lives in Florida. I wouldn't want to wake her and her family this late. I'll reach out to her tomorrow."

"Okay, if you're sure," Brad said. "I'm going to step out for a moment to call Grams to let her know I won't be home until later. I don't want to worry her either."

"Good thinking, young man." Ted patted his hand, and they both looked up when two paramedics came rushing in.

Brad backed away to allow them to check Ted over and took the opportunity to head for the front door. He kept his eyes on the ground to stop anyone from talking to him. He needed to get some fresh air. He tried to remain calm while his stomach rolled like a tilt-a-whirl on full speed. That arm around his throat felt as if it were still squeezing him, and the weight of the barrel's cold metal remained at the side of his head.

Once he cleared the threshold, Brad turned right and headed for Eric's truck. He rounded the hood, away from prying eyes, and took a seat on the chrome bumper. Pain shot through his arm when he attempted to raise his shaky hand to rub his throbbing throat.

He had to keep it together for Ted. The old guy depended on him.

A shadow covered the glow from the streetlight overhead, but Brad didn't even bother to look up. He knew it was Eric.

"How are you?" Eric asked, his voice low and calm.

"Great. I'll be fine. You know, master criminal here. I'm used to danger." Straight-up lie. He'd never once entered a house when he knew someone was there—no face to face. Ever. Brad would be long gone when the owners came home. He'd seen more guns while working at The Gates then he'd ever had when he burglarized other criminals'' homes.

Eric knelt so that they were at eye level with one another. "Not buying it, Bradley." His hands rested on the bumper on either side of Brad, surrounding him with those big arms, which oddly made him feel calmer.

He looked into Eric's dark brown eyes and could feel himself gravitating to the comfort the captain was offering before having to pull himself back forcefully.

Getting used to it would do neither of them any good.

Chapter Five

"Brad," he said as he leaned away from Eric.

"Yes, Bradley." Eric wanted to comfort the skittish man, but he knew he'd have to allow him to make the first move.

"Not Bradley, just Brad."

"Oh, there is nothing 'just' about you, Bradley. You're so much more." If there was one thing Eric was sure of, it was that.

He'd seen trained men who weren't as cool and contained in similar situations. From the moment he had entered the store, he'd known everything Brad had been doing was to protect the old man. Respect didn't begin to cover the emotion that nearly overwhelmed him after the assailant was subdued. Up until that point, Eric had to lock down his feelings to keep his presence unknown until he could take down the perp.

But now? Now that he knew Brad wasn't injured, but was surely shaken, Eric couldn't contain the feelings roiling through him.

Brad sat staring at him as if Eric had grown a second head, but he refused to look away. "What you did in there to protect Ted was heroic whether you choose to believe it or not. If you hadn't stepped in when the owner froze in fear, that guy would've probably killed him."

"You're the one who took him down." Brad tried to deflect the praise away from himself, and Eric wouldn't allow it.

"You distracted him long enough for me to get into position, and you knocked the gun out of his hand," Eric stated. "Face it. You're the hero for the second time in our relationship."

"Relationship?" Brad's eyes widened.

"That was not the point I was trying to make, but yeah, relationship. Back to my point," Eric said. "I was scared in there. It's okay to be scared. There's no shame in that."

"You were scared. Right. You're Captain Cop. This is a normal Thursday for you." Brad buried his face into his hands and groaned.

"It isn't every day that someone I care for is in danger," Eric countered. "So yeah, I was scared."

Brad's head popped back up as if it was on a spring. "You care—care for me?"

"Sure." Why lie?

Before they could take this conversation any further, Sam came around the side of Eric's truck. "They're loading Ted into the ambulance."

Brad stood. "I'm going with him."

Eric rose and crossed his arms over his chest. "You're more than going with Ted. You're getting your throat looked at while we're there."

Brad looked ready to argue, but shook his head instead. "You're coming to the hospital?"

"Damn right, I am." Where the hell else would he be going?

Sam looked between the two of them. "Okay, we'll take your statements after everyone gets checked out."

Brad looked at Eric a bit longer before rolling his eyes and walking away in the direction of the ambulance.

"You want to tell me what that's all about, Captain?" Sam asked with a knowing look.

"No," Eric grunted. "I'll meet you at the hospital."

He walked over to the driver's side of his truck and jumped in. Whatever was happening between him and Brad was no one's business but their own.

***

The ride to the hospital didn't take long, and Brad soon found himself on a gurney beside Ted's. Seriously, Eric had lost his damn mind if he thought Brad was going to lie there like some fainting maid out of one of Grams's romance novels. He swore he'd only read them out of curiosity, not for the great storylines, multidimensional characters, or solid relationships and happy endings. *Honest.*

Brad sat up, threw his legs over the side, and was ready to jump off the gurney when he heard that deep voice.

"Don't even think about it," Eric rumbled.

"Do you have cameras in here, 'cause this shit is scary. You're not even in the room."

Eric came in from the hallway with a grin glued to his face. "I don't have to be in here to know what you're thinking. Now sit back down until we get the results of your scan."

"What about Ted?" Brad asked as he watched the older man pull on his jacket. "He's standing up."

"That's because Ted is going home. Doc said he's cleared to leave now that his memory has returned, and his blood pressure has gone down." Eric crossed his arms again as he often did when he was digging in for an argument.

How am I even aware of his quirks?

"Sorry, Brad," Ted said while walking over to his bedside. "Thank you for what you did for me. You likely saved my life, young man, and I won't forget it. Your Gramps would have been so proud of you. He always was—even through those last few years that he spent in treatment when things got you knocked off track."

Brad glanced at Eric before saying. "Let's not dig up the past in mixed company, Ted."

The older man shook his head. "It's nothing to be ashamed of. You did what you had to do. But I'll respect your wishes."

Eric observed them, and Brad knew the captain was trying to piece together the small bits of information Ted had given. The last thing Brad needed was for him to complete the puzzle. That shit was private.

"I'll walk you out, Ted," Eric said. "Sam's going to give you a ride home, and if you need anything, you have my card."

Ted patted his shirt pocket. "Thank you, Captain Meyers, for everything."

"It's my job," Eric said, and it sounded rehearsed as if it was his standard answer. Sure, being a cop was his job, but his heroic actions were all his own.

"It's more than a job, son," Ted countered. "It's in you to help others. You can't hide that kind of commitment."

Brad watched as they left the room, and for a split second, he considered getting up. However, his neck did hurt, and maybe it was worth finding out if anything was damaged. Not because the captain told him not to move.

Keep telling yourself that.

Brad felt all kinds of messed up inside. Choked out while having a gun jammed against the side of his head. Watching Eric wrestle the attacker to the ground. Then he goes ahead and tells him point-blank that he cares about him. It sounded like a recipe for therapy, and not the physical kind.

How had his day gone from nothing eventful to him having a boyfriend? No, no, no, not a boyfriend, barely a friend, really, an acquaintance for sure, but nope, not boyfriend, or even friends with benefits. Not going to happen.

Brad's thoughts had been going around in circles like a tornado, and he hadn't noticed Eric and the doctor entering his room. Both now stood staring at him.

"You okay, Bradley?" Eric asked as he moved closer to the bed. "I said your name, but you didn't respond."

"No, no, I'm fine," Brad answered. "What do you have for me, Doc?"

The doctor looked down at the tablet he was holding before saying. "You're fortunate, Mr. Williams. The cuts and abrasions to your skin are minor. Damage to your arteries, trachea, and cervical spine are minor as well, but we need to keep an eye on your throat for swelling. You can use icepacks for no more than ten minutes at a time and take acetaminophen for any discomfort. If you find that it's becoming more difficult for you to swallow or breathing becomes labored, come back to the ER."

"Thanks, Doctor Galen," Eric replied.

"Yeah, thank you," Brad said and then suddenly remembered something vital. "Shit, I didn't call Grams. She'll be frantic."

He sat up and tried to jump off the gurney, but again Eric stopped him with a hand to his chest. "Don't worry; I called her while the doctor was examining you. She knows you're okay and that I'll bring you home once we're finished here."

Brad shot an accusing look at Eric. "How did you know I hadn't called her, and why do you have my home number?"

Eric shook his head. "Always so suspicious. You left your cellphone in the truck, and I called Saint for your Grams's number. I didn't want her worrying. In case you forgot, I'm a police captain, and you were involved in a crime. The information is necessary."

Okay, now Brad felt like an idiot. What was wrong with him? The man had done something incredibly kind, and he'd bitten his head off.

"I've already signed your release papers, so you are free to leave anytime," the doctor said before turning and leaving the two of them alone.

Brad rubbed the back of his neck with the palm of his hand. "Look, man, I'm sorry. I shouldn't have jumped all over you like that. It's been a long day."

"After everything, I think you have a right to be on edge," Eric said, smile still in place. "Now, let's get out of this place. Hospitals give me the creeps."

"You're the one that made me come here."

"You were coming along with Ted, remember?"

"Yeah, that's the point. I was coming along, not offering to take up a bed in the ER. That was all on you, buddy." If Brad had it his way, they would have left with Ted.

Eric's smile never faltered once. "Come on, let's get you home."

Brad followed Eric out of the room. They walked down the hall, and to a bank of elevators without saying a word. He couldn't help but admire the way Eric's jeans molded to his muscular butt. *What the hell am I doing?* He was ogling the police captain's ass, and by the smirk on Eric's face, he knew it.

"Shut up," Brad said before pushing the elevator button.

"Didn't say a word, but I could walk slower if you need more time for a longer look."

Brad raked the palm of his hand down his face, and thankfully the elevator doors slid open. "What the hell am I doing?"

"Appreciating all the hard work I put into my glutes. I'm flattered."

Brad stepped onto the elevator, and Eric followed. "Are you gay?" Because knowing his luck, when the captain said he cared for him, he probably meant like a brother. *Oh shit, what if he meant it in an entirely platonic way, and I blew it way out of proportion?*

One moment he was watching the floor numbers count down, the next Brad found himself surrounded. "Yes, I'm gay, and yes, I do care about you more than being your friend."

Eric ran his index finger along Brad's jaw before tilting his head up so that they were looking at each other eye to eye. "Tell me now if you don't have an interest in me."

This was his chance. Shoot the guy down. Keep it simple. No complications. However, the longer he looked into those dark eyes, the more Brad realized how much Eric had come to mean to him over the time they'd known each other.

The longer they stood pressed together, the closer their lips became. Did he want this? Who was he fooling? Hell yeah, he wanted the big guy.

The moment their lips touched, and electricity shot through his body. Those big hands of his cupped the back of Brad's head and held him gently in place while his soft lips explored. A rush of heat flooded his body as his hands roamed over Eric's broad chest. He wanted under the fabric.

The elevator slowed. They were almost on the ground floor. Eric pulled away slightly before running the tip of his tongue along Brad's lower lip as if he needed a final taste before the bell sounded, and the doors slid open.

Twenty minutes later, they were pulling up to Brad's building.

"Are you sure you don't want me to go up with you?" Eric asked before putting his truck into park. "I don't mind."

Brad held his backpack in one hand, and two icepacks in a plastic bag in the other. One of the nurses brought the packs and reminded him no more than ten minutes within an hour's time.

"I'm sure," he replied. "I don't think Grams is expecting company this late."

"Another time," Eric said, sounding disappointed. "Wait." He held out a small paper bag to Brad. "Here."

"What is it?" Brad asked as he took the bag.

"Your Grams's licorice and tickets." Brad looked inside the bag, and sure enough, it was his grandmother's care bag, but not the same items as always. "I didn't know what brands your grandmother liked, so I asked the guy at the hospital's gift shop which was popular."

Brad didn't know what to say. Thank you seemed small in comparison to how he felt about this gesture, but it was all he had. "Thanks. She'll be so happy."

"I think she'll be happier you're okay, but those," he dipped his chin at the bag, "can be the cherry on top of the good news."

Brad nodded. "You can meet her if you'd like next time, on Tuesday," he said as he cracked the passenger door open, flooding the cab with light. "Let me know so I can tell her to expect company." He glanced at Eric. "I guess I'll see you on Tuesday."

"Four days seems too long. When do you work this weekend? Maybe we could get dinner, and I could meet your Grams then."

"You go at one speed, don't you? Full throttle," Brad joked.

"When I know it's right, yeah."

"And this," Brad motioned between the two of them, "is right?" He knew Eric had to realize what he was genuinely asking. The criminal and the cop didn't have a snowball's chance in hell of making this work.

"It is."

Brad thought about it for a moment. "Okay. Call me, I'm working the day shift on Saturday, and I'm off on Sunday."

"I will."

He wanted to lean over and kiss Eric again but decided to jump out of the truck.

Better to take things slow. Brad already had enough "crazy" in his life.

Chapter Six

Rookies were going to be the death of him.

Eric often wondered how they survived the police academy. Another of life's great mysteries. Every now and again, an exceptional new candidate had LAPD written all over him or her. Then, you'd get that "one" who had no business being a cop. Either ineptitude or the wrong temperament, especially the folks who believed being a cop was all about power or high-speed chases. Usually, those assholes ran through new partners until no one was left who wanted to work with them. Always a highlight from these "special" rookies was their belief they knew more than senior officers who'd been on the job before the rookie was born.

Eric found himself with the trifecta this time around. A transfer from another station for whom they couldn't find a long-term position. In other words, "tag, you're it." He's your problem now. Clay Everett had a chip on his shoulder the size of Texas, along with a problem with authority. Seriously? Why become a cop? The PD was a paramilitary organization that insisted on following the rules and the chain of command.

Eric let out a deep breath and closed the file on his new rookie. Who to partner Everett with? It would have to be someone with a large helping of patience and experience—a solid cop who wouldn't take any bullshit. One person sprang to mind: Sam.

Through the glass panels of his office, he spied the man in question. Without hesitation, Eric lifted his phone and dialed Sam's extension.

"Web here," he answered.

"Sam, can I see you in my office when you have a moment?" Eric asked.

"Sure thing, Cap."

Eric hung up and watched as Sam typed something onto his keyboard before standing and heading toward Eric's office. He knew how his friend and colleague would take the news. This rookie already had a rep and came with a warning label.

Eric waved Sam to come in before he had a chance to knock on the door.

"You wanted to talk to me, sir?" Sam asked as he stuck his head past the door's frame.

"Yeah. Come in."

Sam shut the door, and sat down in one of the two chairs set in front of Eric's tidy desk. "What's up, Cap?"

Eric didn't do stuffy, but he thought adherence to certain formalities imbued respect, which officers with rank earned and deserved. Looking at the self-assured man lounging with his arm over the back of the chair, Eric realized something. "Suddenly, I'm not so torn up about assigning you your new partner."

Sam shot straight up. "What? Wait, I'm good on my own."

"Not anymore. You know it's much safer having two officers in each squad car. It was only a matter of time until we replaced your old partner when he retired," Eric explained.

"It's only been a couple of months," Sam countered.

"Closer to nine months, buddy. I can't hold this off any longer." Eric was well aware that Sam and his last partner had been a team for three years, and that change was hard.

"Fine. Who's the lucky cop?"

"This just keeps getting easier," Eric chuckled while watching his cocky friend. "Clay Everett, he's being transferred over from West Bureau."

"Transferred?" Sam sat even straighter in his chair. "Why?"

Eric looked at Sam and grinned. "He's had some difficulty adjusting."

"Adjusting? He's a rookie, and he's been transferred already? C'mon, Cap. Don't do this to me."

"Sam, you're the best chance I have at figuring out what's up with this guy. Your patience has no bounds, you're a likable guy, but you don't take anyone's shit." Eric couldn't help but chuckle again as the word brought up images of Clay's former partner locked in a pungent PortaPotty at a construction site on Wilshire Boulevard. Apparently, Everett thought he was pulling a harmless prank. He'd gotten off light with a formal warning, but the fact his captain requested Everett be transferred told a bigger tale.

"This may be funny for you, but you owe me," Sam snapped.

"I know."

"And if I end up with a bullet in my ass, you're going take leave and become my in-home care worker."

Eric laughed. "Agreed."

"Hazardous duty pay. I need hazardous duty pay."

"Ah, no."

"Damn it," Sam grumbled. "I'll play nice." Sam rubbed the back of his neck. "When's he arriving?"

"Monday, at seven a.m. You'll be back on days until we figure out what to do with him."

"Well, at least I'll be able to have dinner with Joey every night." Sam cracked the first smile Eric saw since Sam learned he had a new "special" partner.

"See, you're already looking on the bright side of this."

"Speaking of bright sides, I hear you've got yourself a date tonight." Sam relaxed back into his chair.

It didn't surprise Eric that Sam would know. Sam's man, Joey, worked with Brad at The Gates. The two were close friends.

"Yeah, I do." No reason to keep it under wraps. He was looking forward to having Brad to himself for a couple of hours.

"That's it? That's all you're giving me?" Sam huffed. "At least tell me where you're taking him."

"I've decided on a place that was laid back and would be fun. Highland Park Bowl." Eric had been trying to pick the perfect place since dropping Brad off on Thursday night.

"The place over on Figueroa Street?" Sam asked. "What about his injured arm?"

"Thought of that. Since Bradley's left-handed and his arm's still healing, he could bowl with his right. I'll bowl with my left since I'm right-handed, to make it fair." He'd wanted something laid-back but upscale, and the renovated steampunk-styled bowling alley seemed like it'd be a fun place. They had a bar and served food as well, so everything was covered.

Sam stared at him like Eric had grown two heads. "You know both of you are going to look like eight-year-olds with all the gutter balls you'll be throwing."

Eric grinned. "I know. Fun, huh?"

"Yeah, all right. It sounds like a great idea. I might take Joey there some time." His smile returned at the mention of his man.

"How's Joey doing?" Eric asked.

"Much better now that all that shit with his grandfather is finally over."

Joey's grandfather was a mobster with a large crime syndicate. Psychotically cruel, he'd had his men hunt down Joey, and kidnapped him with the intention of removing one of his kidneys in a fucked-up attempt at saving his son, Joey's uncle's, life. Brad had helped them rescue Joey from his grandfather's fortified mansion.

"May the man rot in hell," Eric said. There was no love lost in the LAPD for that asshole. The man had personally killed, and ordered killed, hundreds of people in his lifetime, and would've killed his grandson to get what he wanted. "Any updates on Joey's condition?" Eric knew Joey's sickle cell disease made everyday life almost impossible at times.

"His new hematologist has him on a different drug that's supposed to lower the number of pain crises he has. If it works, I'd be grateful. It guts me to see him in pain, and there's nothing I can do to help him."

"I couldn't imagine being in either of your positions. The amount of strength the two of you show every day is amazing."

"Joey's the amazing one," Sam said proudly. "The man is unstoppable."

"That he is."

***

"Why did I ever agree to this?"

"Because you like the man, that's why." Grams's amused voice floated down the hallway from the living room.

Brad looked at himself in the full-length mirror that hung on the back of the bathroom door. Eric had said they were going somewhere casual, so Brad thought his dark-washed jeans and a vintage tee would do. He didn't have much clothing, and he didn't date. This choosing-an-outfit shit was making him crazy.

"What's 'like' got to do with it? This date is going to be a disaster." Yet he couldn't deny his excitement at the thought of going on a date with Eric.

"Disaster? Please," she said, much closer this time, making Brad jump.

He opened the bathroom door to find his Grams standing, with the help of her walker, on the other side. "Stop sneaking up on me."

"I wasn't sneaking. You're not paying attention because you're all worked up over your date. Now let me see what you're wearing."

Brad opened the door up the rest of the way and stood there feeling like a loser while his grandmother inspected him before his date. "He said it's casual."

Grams smiled wide. "You look so handsome. The captain would be crazy if he didn't make a move on you."

"Grams," Brad groaned. "You're not supposed to be thinking that stuff at your age."

"My age? I'll have you know your grandfather and I—"

"Stop," he yelled while covering his ears. "I don't want to hear about whatever you and Gramps did. Are you trying to scar me for life?"

Grams laughed and sat down on her walker's plastic seat. "After everything this family has gone through, I doubt anything I say would even make it into the scarring territory, young man."

Brad nodded. She had a point. "True enough, but I still don't want to hear about it."

"Oh, shush." Grams swatted his arm. "Don't you get smart with me. Now take this."

She held out her hand, her fingers closed, concealing what she was holding. "Gee, now I feel like I'm going to the prom. There better not be a boutonniere in there."

She laughed. Since Gramps had died, Brad had made it his mission to keep her happy. No matter what. "You wouldn't be caught dead at a high school prom."

"Again, true. So whatcha got for me?"

Grams opened her arthritic fingers, revealing something Brad hadn't seen in many years. His grandfather's gold signet ring. The last time he'd seen it had been when he visited Gramps in the hospital the day before he'd passed away. He could still make out the Coat of Arms engraved into the oval.

The ring was handed down over centuries of the Williams clan. When he was young, his Gramps would tell him stories about their ancestors who hailed from Scotland. He was proud that their family line traced back to before Robert the Bruce became the King of Scotland.

"I thought Gramps's ring had been buried with him?" He had never given it a second thought.

"It was never his ring to keep," she said in a near whispered. "This belongs to the clan. To be carried down through the generations of Williams originating from the shire of Inverness in the Northwest Highlands. Which means it is yours to care for until there comes a time for you to hand it down to the next generation."

Brad didn't know what to say, but he had a question. "Why have you waited for years to give this to me?"

"Since your grandfather's death, you've been lost, dear. You had spent years doing everything you could think of to save his life, and it felt like a part of you had died when he did."

She was right. Since Gramps's death, every part of him had changed. His entire reason to get up every day and steal was so he could save his grandfather by paying for expensive treatments. That Brad ended up losing him to cancer anyway had nearly done Brad in.

Of course, he loved his Grams with the same ferocity, but he no longer believed that throwing money at treatment would stop death when it came for you. It had been a hard pill to swallow at the time, but a couple of years later, he had come to terms with a reality no one enjoyed learning.

"I agree. It's been a tough couple of years," he said before taking the worn piece of gold into his shaking hand. "Why now?"

Her expression softened. "Your grandfather was a smart man, always had been, it's what attracted me to him all those years ago. He told me to wait until I was sure you'd moved past his death. That way, this ring would be a happy gift and not a constant reminder he was no longer with us. You have a good job, friends, and you're dating, all signs leading me to believe that you have moved past the pain."

Brad rubbed the pad of his thumb over the engraving, worn down by generations of ancestors doing the same thing. It might be crazy, but at that moment, he could feel his Gramps once again. If there was such a thing as spirits, Gramps was definitely with the two of them right then.

He had to swallow past the lump in his throat before saying, "Thanks for saving this for me. Love you, Grams." He followed his clumsy gratitude with a hug, full of the happiness of good memories.

Now, finding the correct finger the band would fit on was another matter. Gramps had large hands with knobby knuckles. He'd worn the ring on his pinky finger. On Brad, it fit his right ring finger. He remembered those big hands picking him up as a child, and how safe they used to make him feel.

It was true, the years had made the bite of his death less severe, and now Brad could see this memento for what it was—a happy memory.

A knock on the front door brought both of them back to the present time.

Eric.

Brad began to panic. He hadn't had a date in years. What if he screwed it up? What if Eric discovered he wasn't that interesting or decided dating a former thief wasn't worth it?

Brad heard voices and realized while he was considering his "what ifs," Grams had gone back to the front of the apartment, and had answered the door. Quickly he shut the bathroom door and began pacing the four-foot space. What was he doing? Hiding? Brad had never hidden from anything in his life. He faced everything head on. His parents' abandonment, his gramps's illness, and forging a new life after losing his grandfather.

The ring on his finger began to warm as he spun it anxiously. He looked down and traced the sword engraved into the center of the coat of arms. He was a Williams who came from a long line of brave men before him, and here he was cowering in a bathroom. The thought of his heritage gave him the strength to do this. He wanted the captain's attention, and there was nothing wrong with that.

With one final look in the mirror, Brad took a deep breath and opened the door. Figuratively and physically.

Chapter Seven

Eric's pants slid against the plastic-covered flowered couch while Grams—as he'd been ordered to call her—sat in what looked to be a well-crafted antique chair.

"So, you want to date my grandson?" she asked him with a sharp look.

She had to know Brad was gay, right? "Yes, I do." Or was this his coming-out moment? Damn.

"You seem like a nice enough fellow," she said.

"Thank you?" He wasn't sure how to respond to that one.

"I see you like my favorite chair. You keep looking at it. Brad gave it to me when we were going through a difficult time." She stroked the worn wood with her pale hand.

"It's a nice chair. Seventeenth-century?" He was confident it wasn't a reproduction.

"You have a good eye," she said with one brow arched.

"More like having a mother who loves antiques."

"Ah, I see," she said while leaning forward, closer to him. "If you have a problem with what Brad did years ago, you best leave him alone."

There was the strong woman who took in her grandson from birth and raised him as her own. He'd suspected he'd have to get past Grams first, and he'd been right.

"I understand what he's told me was done in the past."

"Understanding is not accepting, young man."

"How can I accept something without knowing any of the details?"

Grams sat back in her chair. "He hasn't told you the whole story?"

"No. The only bit I know is that Bradley's been retired from his previous profession for the past couple years and no longer burglarizes the city's less-than-savory crowd's homes." Eric was honest. That was all he knew about Brad's former career. Of course, he wanted to know more, but he was leaving the timing of that up to Brad.

"Interesting," she continued. "And you still came to take him out on a date, even not knowing the truth."

"I don't believe Bradley is a bad person. I've based my decisions on his behavior now, not in the past," Eric explained.

"You're a strange cop. I thought most of you believed once a criminal, always a criminal."

"Not all of us see it that way." While it was true others believed certain people couldn't be rehabilitated, Eric didn't subscribe to that thinking.

"See what, what way?" Brad asked as he entered the room from the hallway.

Eric stood. Brad looked good in his tight jeans and a vintage t-shirt. Had he ever seen Brad dressed in anything other than his bartending uniform or shorts and a workout shirt? Then it hit him that Brad had asked a question, but before Eric could answer, Grams took over.

"That the Dodgers haven't got a prayer of making it into the playoffs."

Brad smiled at his Grams. "Are you grilling him about baseball? Not everyone has an obsession with the Dodgers like you do."

He walked over and kissed the older woman on her cheek before turning toward Eric. Those hazel eyes took their time looking him up and down before resting on his face.

"You look handsome tonight," Brad said before a look of shock crossed his face as if he hadn't meant to say that out loud.

Eric wasn't about to let him feel uncomfortable for one moment. "Thank you, so do you, Bradley. Ready to go?"

Brad relaxed, and his smile returned. Perfect.

"Yeah. Where we going?"

"If I told you, it wouldn't be a surprise." Eric laughed as Brad placed both of his hands on his hips in mock anger. "Let's go. I'm starving." He took hold of Brad's hand before turning toward Grams. "It was a pleasure meeting you."

"You as well, Eric. You're welcome here anytime." She gave a decisive nod before continuing. "If you're not going to make it home, please let me know so I don't worry."

"Grams." Brad huffed and lowered his head in what Eric could assume was embarrassment.

"Don't worry, Grams. I'll make sure he calls."

Brad's head sprang back up. "Grams?"

"Yes." Grams nodded. "I've asked your friend here to call me by that name." She patted Brad's arm. "Now, go have fun and leave me to my scratch tickets."

"You brought her scratch tickets?" Brad's hands returned to his sides.

Eric shrugged.

"And black licorice," Grams sing-songed while picking up a quarter from her side table.

"Suck up," Brad grumbled while trying to contain a smirk.

"Guilty as charged," Eric admitted. "I figured since I'm taking out her grandson, I'd better bring gifts."

"Smart man," she stated, head bent over a scratcher.

"Good to know that all someone has to do is bring your favorites to buy you off." Brad couldn't contain his chuckle.

"No, not someone. Him." Grams raised her head and pointed at Eric, who wiggled his eyebrows at Bradley.

Brad grabbed his hand more forcefully than necessary and began leading them to the front door. "Now the two of you are teaming up. This doesn't bode well for my continued sanity."

He barely slowed down to open the door before pulling Eric through and into the apartment building's hallway. Eric could still hear Grams laughing as Brad locked the door behind him.

As soon as he turned, Eric pinned him to the closed door and ran his thumb along Brad's jaw. "Hi." He lowered his lips to Brad's and dove in like a starving man. He'd been thinking about the kiss they shared on Thursday night to the point of distraction.

Eric slowed the kiss and looked down at Brad's flushed face. His eyes were still closed, and his soft lips parted. "God, you're beautiful."

As soon as those hazel eyes opened, Eric took his hand and led him down the hallway to the elevators. He couldn't wait to get this date started.

***

Brad felt as though he was seeing a whole new side of Eric tonight. He was still totally controlling, but there was an excitement radiating off him that Brad had never seen before.

Eric held the truck's passenger door open, and as soon as Brad sat, he began buckling him in. Brad had become fond of this gesture of care. He felt special, but he had to be honest. "You don't have to do up my seatbelt anymore. I've gained a lot of my mobility back in my left arm since starting PT."

It seemed like the big guy thought about it for a moment before saying, "I'd still like to continue doing it, if that's okay with you."

So maybe he wasn't the only one fond of their truck ritual. "I'd...I'd like that."

That sexy smile lit up Eric's face as he leaned forward and stole a quick kiss before shutting the door. The more they kissed, the more Brad wanted them to keep going. His libido was in overdrive, and he blamed it on the fact that he hadn't had a date, or even a hookup, in over eleven months.

As they pulled out, Brad realized that for the first time in years, he was doing something completely normal. Not breaking codes, dismantling security systems, or praying that this time would be the last time he'd have to steal before he got caught. Tonight, he was like everyone else. It was Saturday night, and he had a date.

Eric reached over and took Brad's hand while concentrating on driving. Brad had butterflies doing synchronized maneuvers in his stomach. He'd never felt uncertain or nervous while ripping off criminals. However, with the feel of this man's calloused hand wrapped around his, Brad had all the calm of a class of four-year-olds on a field trip.

They were driving into Little Tokyo, one of Brad's favorite places in the city. Amazing restaurants with authentic food. He hoped they were going to a sushi place.

"I hear you thinking," Eric said. "I don't want you to be nervous. I'll tell you if you wish."

Surprise. To save him from being anxious, Eric was willing to break his word and tell Brad where they were going.

There was a sweet side to the captain that Brad doubted many people saw, and he felt honored to be in that exclusive group. "Nope, I'm going to wait for my surprise."

Eric's smile was genuinely happy. "I'd hoped you'd say that."

With another squeeze to his hand, Brad watched the lights of DTLA sparkle around them. He preferred the night. The pavement glowed under the streetlights, and cold steel buildings warmed from the glow within. Older worn buildings of stone softened in the pool of the streetlights as the day's harsh sunlight gave way to mystery and glamor. If he had to choose, Brad felt most comfortable in the night than he ever had during the day.

Cat burglar. Remember?

The truck slowed as they took an off-ramp from the highway and turned onto a surface street. People were walking down the sidewalks on both sides of the street. A person could get lost here if they wanted, and recreate themselves into someone new. For all his grumbling about traffic, rude people, and noise, Brad loved living in LA.

Eric slowed, and up the street, Brad could make out a large, red sign with white letters glowing against the worn stone façade and peeling paint of a building. He couldn't be serious, could he?

"Bowling?" he asked.

"Yep, bowling. Don't judge the place by the outside. It's all renovated and restored into a steampunk bar, restaurant, bowling alley. Actually, during prohibition, this place had doctors upstairs writing patient prescriptions for whiskey that they filled downstairs while enjoying a game or two."

That was an impressive history, and it did have Brad's curiosity piqued, but he had to say something. "I know I said my arm is better, but I don't think I'm ready for bowling."

Eric's smile didn't waver. "Of course not. To make it fair, I'll bowl with my left hand, while you use your right. I've reserved a lane for a couple of hours, and we can choose how much actual bowling happens. In the meantime, I figured we could order some food and drinks and get to know each other better."

Eric surprised Brad again, though he shouldn't have been. Eric had been showing his care and concern pretty much from day one.

Both of them bowling with their less dominant hands. This should be good. Casual, friendly, and no pressure. "I'm in."

"I knew you would be." Eric grinned. "Let's check the place out. We'll find a parking spot, and we'll head inside."

"You've never been here either?"

"No. I've seen pictures online, and I've heard it's a blast and the food's great, but never set foot inside though I've wanted to. Until now, I've never really had a good reason."

Brad wasn't sure what to say. He was the "good reason." Well, hell. Knowing this should've made him anxious over screwing up the evening, but, surprisingly, he felt grounded. Eric saw something in him that Brad hadn't seen in himself. But, now that he thought about it, he deserved to have a good time. He worked hard—yeah, he dropped more glasses than he should—but he also took care of his grandmother, and had kept his nose clean.

Tonight, Brad was joining the land of the living. Regular people who didn't question whether they should go out with friends, throw back a beer, and go bowling.

Eric turned off the ignition, jumped out, and came around the front of the truck. He opened Brad's door and held out his hand. "Ready?"

Let the games begin.

Chapter Eight

The touch of Eric's hand on his lower back sent waves of warmth through Brad's body as Eric guided him down the sidewalk toward the bowling alley.

When they stepped inside, the image of a circa 1990's fiberglass and neon-covered alley with glow-in-the-dark bowling his grandparents had taken him to when he was a kid was the complete opposite of what was before him.

This bowling alley screamed "adult," from the tufted, brown leather couches, to the funky chandeliers in the hallway on their way into the building. There were eight lanes, open straight to the pinsetters at the back so the players could watch the pins reset. Bowling balls returned above ground, in between the lanes. The place was designed using wood, open rafters, dark metals, leather, and statement lighting like the pinsetter chandelier over the bar. Most of it looked original. They even had bowling leagues, and old pennants hung on the wall, some dating back to 1927. The balls had imprinted on them "Bowl for your health."

The smell of wood-fired pizza wafted passed him, making Brad's mouth water. The place was busy. There were a lot of people, bowling, eating, or socializing around the oval bar. Eric had been right. This place did give off a steampunk vibe, and was cool.

They stopped off at the bar, and Brad noticed Eric was watching him closely. "What do you think?"

"It amazing. This place has a cool vibe and tons of character. I like it."

Eric beamed. "I thought you would. From what I've heard, no one comes here and doesn't have a good time."

"I could see hanging out here," Brad agreed.

Before Eric could answer, a bartender came over to them.

"Hey. You gonna wait for a hi-top, or are you sitting at the bar?"

"I have a reservation for one of the lanes," Eric answered.

"Go ahead and get checked in. Then you can order from the lane."

With his hand against Brad's lower back, Eric ushered him to the bowling shoes stacked in individual cubbies. As Eric took care of their check-in, Brad continued to look around. The worn wood on the ball returns fit in with the couches and black wrought-iron of the table legs and bases. Around the outsides of the lanes stood small tables for two behind railings on two stories. Closer to the bar, the tables were larger than those by the lanes.

Eric called, "What size shoe are you, Bradley?"

"Ten and a half."

"Got it."

Moments later, they were sitting on the couch in front of their lane, changing into the multicolored bowling shoes while menus sat on the coffee table in front of them ready for their perusal.

Brad looked over at the handsome man beside him and said, "Thanks. This place is exactly what I need, even if I didn't know I needed it."

Eric reached over and ran his hand down Brad's back. "I'm glad. We'll come here again then."

Brad couldn't help the excitement at the thought that this date wasn't a one-off. There was going to be more.

They both ordered a draft and decided on a large Margherita pizza.

"So, what do you think?" Eric asked as he motioned toward the bowling balls. "Want to give it a try?"

"You ready to get your ass kicked?" Brad asked in return. "I used to be a pretty good bowler back in the day when the three of us went out."

"Your grandparents and you?" Eric asked.

"Yeah," he responded and couldn't help but smile at the memory. "Every Sunday after church. Gramps used to say, first we praise, then afterward, if we had any frustrations leftover, we take them out on the pins. Both Grams and Gramps played in leagues in Pasadena. All week we worked hard, but Sunday was our day for the three of us." The memory was comforting and painful.

"Sounds like you had a lot of fun," Eric said. "What did your grandparents do for a living?"

Brad took a drink of his beer and sat it back down on the table. "They owned a tailoring shop not far from our building. The shop had been in the family since my grams's parents."

"What happened to it?"

"Gramps got sick. He was diagnosed with lung cancer though he never smoked a day in his life."

"I'm so sorry, Bradley," Eric said, his deep voice sounding sad.

"He passed away two years ago. Grams couldn't run the shop on her own no matter how much I helped, and then she began to develop arthritis in her hands." It seemed like they were hit by one blow after another that year.

"I noticed how hard a time she had picking up the quarter to scratch her tickets."

"Yeah, that was the beginning of the end. Gramps got sicker and was spending much more time in the hospital, and Grams couldn't keep up the shop and care for him, so she closed it down."

Brad would have done anything to have kept that shop for her. But between its expensive upkeep and the medical bills piling up, there was no way to save it. Eric sat, listening to him carefully. Other than with Grams, Brad never talked about his past with anyone. It felt freeing to tell Eric, who was a good listener, but Brad didn't want to lay it all out while they were on a date.

"How about we give this opposite-hand bowling a try?"

"Let's do this," Eric agreed without missing a beat, allowing the subject to be dropped in favor of happier pursuits. "You want to go first?"

"Sure." They both stood, and Brad stepped up to the ball return, where he noticed each of the balls had written on them, "Tonight We Bowl." Yeah, cool as fuck.

The ball felt odd in this hand. He'd never bowled right-handed and regretted ever admitting he knew how to bowl. "This might be embarrassing. I'm not sure about my control doing it this way, but I'm willing to give it a try."

"That's what I thought you'd say. You're not a 'give up' kind of guy. I'm gonna be in the same boat. Worst case, we'll both bowl horrible games."

Brad stepped up to their lane as Eric sat on the couch. He loosened his grip slightly because the tips of his fingers were going numb. He could do this. He tried to remember everything he'd done when he used to bowl with his grandparents. Same motion, only he was using the other hand.

He brought the ball up in front of him and stepped forward, swinging his right arm back, gaining momentum. As he brought the ball forward, he released it down the center of the lane. Excellent.

Whatever confidence he had quickly faded as the ball slid off to the side and fell into the right gutter roughly halfway down the lane. He couldn't remember the last time he'd thrown a gutter ball. Instead of being disappointed, he couldn't help but be happy.

He turned back to Eric and burst out laughing at the look of concern on his face. Brad had no idea how badly he'd missed bowling and all the happy memories it brought back, gutter ball and all.

"I think I'm rusty. I might need a little work," he said between laughs.

Eric smiled wide, and Brad walked up to stand in front of him. He had no idea where his bold attitude was coming from, but he dipped down and snuck a kiss before retrieving his ball from the return.

Tonight was going to be fantastic.

***

Eric watched as ball after ball sunk into the gutters. It seemed that neither of them could bowl with their non-dominant hands. But it didn't seem to matter. They laughed and joked as they ate their pizza, oblivious to the other people playing and talking around them. This evening was the first time in a long time that he'd let down his guard and laughed until his sides hurt.

Their reservation was almost at an end, but he didn't want the date to be over so soon. He wondered if it was too early in their relationship to invite Brad back to his apartment, even if it didn't involve sex. Eric decided not to bring it up. He'd wait for Brad to become more comfortable with him first.

Brad finished the last of his coffee and turned to Eric. "So, what do you have planned for us after this?"

Okay, maybe he was already comfortable. "I could take you home, or we could go back to my place and watch a little television and relax."

"I'm going with curtain number two, Bob."

Eric couldn't help but pull the man in for a hug. He was one of a kind.

Eric paid the check and led Brad to the outside door. They walked through and were back out on the sidewalk. The air was a bit cooler now.

"Where do you live?"

"Silver Lake," Eric said. "I rent a two-bedroom bungalow." They stopped alongside his truck as he unlocked the door.

"Wow, that's an expensive neighborhood. I didn't know a cop's salary went that high."

"It doesn't. I lucked out years ago when I first moved from NorCal. An older widow owns the property, and she lives in the house next door. She liked the idea of having a police officer around and rented it to me at a reasonable price. I cut our lawns and do all the exterior upkeep, as well as handyman duties, so she doesn't have to hire anyone, which, combined with the rent I pay, makes it a good deal for her."

"Win-win."

"Exactly," Eric said while opening Brad's door. "I'll give you a tour of the place when we get there."

"Cool."

Brad jumped into the truck, and Eric reached in and secured his seatbelt. He liked the idea of making sure Brad was safe, with the extra benefit of stealing a kiss while he leaned over the sexy man.

Within moments, they were on their way to his home. Tonight would be the first time he'd ever brought a date back to his place. Between never having met anyone he wanted in his house, and keeping his life on the DL because of his fucked-up relationship with his stepfather, Eric took a beat to realize this was a momentous occasion.

What was it about Brad that made Eric throw caution to the wind and bask in this happiness?

He didn't have an answer, but he was sticking around to find out.

Chapter Nine

On the drive over to Eric's house, without a word, Eric had grabbed Brad's hand and placed it on his thigh. Brad waited for Eric to say something, but he kept his eyes on the road. The sky had turned dark, and Brad thought it might be a good time to let Grams in on the new plan.

"I'm going to text Grams to let her know that I might be a bit later, so she doesn't worry." Brad wondered if he sounded like a teenager, but he loved his Grams, and she'd been through enough. He would never intentionally make her worry.

"Good idea," Eric said. "She'll appreciate that."

Brad pulled out his phone and shot off a quick message. Seconds later, his phone beeped with her reply. ***Have fun, sweetheart. Spend the night if you want. I'm going to bed soon anyway.*** A heart emoji followed it.

Spend the night. *Does she think her grandson is that easy?*

He glanced over at Eric's handsome profile. His soft lips were slightly parted, and the headlights from the oncoming vehicles highlighted his strong jaw and cheekbones. Add in those dark, mysterious eyes and thick hair into the mix, and Brad couldn't help but think that Eric looked like a silent film hero brought to life in the twenty-first century.

On second thought, maybe Brad was that easy, because damn, he was tempted to do everything spending the night entailed.

"Why are you staring at me?" Eric asked with a big grin on his face.

Shit. Busted.

There was no way he was going to add to Eric's already "healthy" ego. "I thought I saw a few grey hairs shining from around your ears in the street lights."

"Asshole," Eric laughed and squeezed his hand. "You'll always keep me grounded."

Brad shrugged. He was never one for lavishing compliments. Of course, he'd compliment people who deserved it, but he didn't hand them out like bumper stickers to people who needed validation through their looks, clothes, or money. To him, compliments were like love: you didn't go throwing it around.

Other than his Grams and Gramps, Brad had never told anyone that he loved them. So far, he'd trusted no one outside his family with something that important.

The truck slowed as they entered what Brad assumed was Eric's neighborhood. The stucco houses on either side of the street ranged in colors and sizes, but all were tidy and clean. Fan palms, pygmy palms, and queen palms grew in almost every yard. Some had grass, while others xeriscaped with stone.

There were vehicles in the driveways, and a large number had detached garages. Definitely what realtors called a "good neighborhood." Silver Lake was known for its artisanal coffee shops, vegan cafés, Asian restaurants, and trendy boutiques. Brad had been there a few times to take in some indie music, and he'd stopped in a couple of its bars.

"You like?" Eric asked as he slowed and turned into the driveway of an adorable sand-colored bungalow. The house looked freshly painted, and the landscaping seemed to highlight the house even further.

"It's beautiful. All of it, the neighborhood and the houses. Who knew you were a hipster?" Eric laughed.

Acting like he hadn't intentionally poked the captain, Brad asked, "Which house belongs to your landlady?"

"That one, to the right," Eric said as he looked out the front windshield.

Brad should have guessed, as the exterior was similar to Eric's. He took good care of the properties. A large window sat on a front step beside a door painted navy blue, adding more character to an already charming neighborhood. Brad wondered if Eric had chosen his front door color or if his landlady had.

Eric shut the truck off and asked, "Want to take a look inside?"

"Definitely," Brad answered, making the big guy smile and jump out of the vehicle.

Brad waited as he came around the front of the truck and opened his door. "Thank you." He took hold of Eric's hand and stepped out.

Brad could hear coyotes howling in the distance, and he smirked. Only in LA. He'd take the distant reminder of who was here first over his few encounters with guard dogs. Eric wrapped his arm around Brad's waist and pulled him closer as they made their way to a side entrance to the house off the driveway, near the detached garage.

Once inside, Eric turned on the lights, revealing Brad's first look at the private side of the captain. The furniture was large, like him, with a leather couch and chair, much like the ones back at the bowling alley, worn and comfortable. What looked to be a new entertainment unit stood against the far wall holding a large television, a few trophies and awards, pictures, and a gaming system. The window he'd seen when they'd pulled up was to the left of the couch and covered by roll-down wood shutters.

On the terracotta-tiled floor sat a brightly colored rug in blue, yellow, and black geometric shapes. Two extra chairs bracketed the couch and beyond Brad could see a kitchen through the arched opening. There was no clutter or frills. The room was functional with a touch of color, but unadorned.

"I like the way you've decorated your living room," he said. "You can get comfortable in here."

"That's what I wanted. A place to relax and unwind that wasn't too busy," Eric explained. "You want to see the rest of the house?"

Brad nodded.

The kitchen looked like it still had the original off-white tiles, some of which had dark blue daisy-like flowers with orange centers. The stove and oven below were old and narrow, which was necessary in the small galley kitchen. Beside the kitchen was a tiny laundry room with a full-size stacked washer/dryer. Small handmade shelves held a few laundry supplies, and there was barely enough room for one person to turn around in the cramped space.

Down the narrow hall was a bathroom with dark and light green tiling—had to be original too—and two bedrooms. The second bedroom was small, and had a narrow sofa Brad guessed folded out to a bed, and a small desk, on top of which was a laptop and a stack of papers. Eric's room had a queen-sized mattress. No way would a king fit in this room unless Eric took out his dresser and the side table. Brad figured Eric slept diagonally on the bed to keep his feet from hanging over the edge.

The functionality mimicked the living room, and everything was tidy and comfortable with the odd splash of color and pictures. Brad thought the home was an accurate representation of a man whose job was messy, noisy, and sometimes tragic. A neat and organized house that provided comfort and ease had to help Eric achieve peace of mind when he was off duty.

They ended the tour back in the living room. "Have a seat," Eric said before picking up the remote from the coffee table and handing it to Brad. "Take a look at the guide and see if there is anything that interests you. I'll grab us some drink and snacks."

"What do you like?" Brad asked. He didn't want to make Eric sit through something he had no interest in watching.

"Comedy, action, mystery, a rom-com. A pretty wide range, so don't worry about me, I'm likely to be happy with your choice," he said, shrugging.

"You always this easy to get along with?"

"My mother might disagree," Eric chuckled.

"Do you get to see much of her?"

"She and Dan come out every couple of months, and I go to Florida whenever I have a chance to visit."

"That's important. I don't know what I would have done without my Grams."

Eric came over to stand in front of him and cupped his cheek in one of his big hands. "And she wouldn't have known what to do without you. You're an important person too. Remember that, please." He lowered his head and took Brad's lips in a deep kiss. Their tongues dueled and explored without hurry, as their bodies molded to one another.

Eric tasted of coffee and mint, and Brad wanted more. Slipping his hands underneath the hem of Eric's shirt became essential. Brad had to feel skin over all that glorious muscle. Eric moaned when Brad ran the palms of his hands over Eric's ripped abs on his way up to his broad chest. His nipples were peaked, and Brad squeezed them.

"Careful, or I might whisk you to the bedroom and keep you there," Eric groaned in pleasure.

"Whisk away," Brad muttered. He wanted Eric so badly that his body was humming in excitement. Every nerve ending was on fire.

Eric looked down at him as if to make sure he'd heard him correctly. "You sure?"

"Hell, yeah."

Eric yanked Brad to his feet, put him flush against Eric's rock-hard body, and walked him backwards down the hall, while staring down at Brad as if he was Eric's next meal. He backed Brad into the bedroom until his legs hit the bed, then Eric pushed Brad's shoulders and he fell onto the mattress.

Eric leaned over, put his huge hands under Brad's armpits and shifted him—the guy was shit strong—until his head hit pillow. Then Eric crawled up and covered Brad. Eric looked like he was ready to do push-ups as he held his upper body off Brad's.

An invitation if Brad ever saw one, he pushed Eric's shirt up so that he could get a better look at what he'd dreamed about. Trimmed, black hair covered Eric's broad chest and led down over his rippled abs and into his jeans.

Brad wanted in those jeans.

"Like what you see?" Eric asked with a knowing smirk.

"It's a fixer-upper, but I'm down for the challenge."

Eric laughed, shaking the entire bed. "Smartass."

"You want me any other way?" Brad said in a joking manner, but part of him wanted to know.

"Nope. I like it or I wouldn't've gone after it."

Before Brad could process those words, Eric dipped his head down and captured Brad's mouth with a blistering kiss. Damn, the man's tongue dueled and danced, pushing Brad to respond in kind. When he thought he couldn't breathe from the intensity, Eric's soft, lush lips trailed down Brad's neck to his collarbone, where he wrapped his teeth around the bone and bit down.

Shit-hot. Brad hadn't had anyone ever do that before and he couldn't wait to feel and see what else Eric would do.

Eric yanked off Brad's shirt and ran his hands over his chest and stomach. He wasn't nearly as toned as Eric, but his hungry smile said he was happy with what he saw.

"You're fuckin' perfect," Eric growled.

Brad's entire body flushed. He'd never had someone compliment him like that. It felt special. The whole night had been. From spending time with Eric and getting to know him, to have the man all to himself in this moment. It'd been one highlight after another.

Eric continued his exploration by unbuttoning Brad's jeans before crawling to the end of the mattress. Pulling off Brad's pants and underwear caused his hard cock to slap against his stomach. Seconds later, the big man stood and began undressing. Shirt off, his gorgeous torso was revealed, all hard angles and muscle.

Brad knew Eric was serious about keeping fit, but there were some excellent genes involved in the sculpting of the masterpiece in front of him.

Brad pushed up onto his elbows to watch the rest of the show. Eric undid the button on his jeans and slowly unzipped them. The tease made Brad's mouth dry as his cock bobbed on his stomach.

"Torture," Brad groaned.

The smile he received was filled with the promise of things to come. He followed the trail of dark hair to his prize and wasn't disappointed. Oh, yeah. Everything on this man was beautiful. Eric removed his jeans and tossed them onto the pile of clothing before crawling back up the bed to position himself above Brad.

The heat from Eric's body scorched Brad's skin. He wrapped his legs around Eric's thick thighs and ran his fingers through his short, dark hair. Those dark eyes seemed to be drinking him in, making Brad warm from the inside out.

In one smooth movement, Eric flipped their positions, and arranged Brad on top of him. "That's better. Now my hands are free to roam all over you."

Brad pushed himself up, positioning Eric's hard cock to slide between the cheeks of Brad's ass. Combing his fingers through Eric's chest hair made him moan, which was one fucking sexy sound.

Brad explored Eric's chest, tweaking his nipples, running his fingers along the ridges of Eric's ridged abs, delighting in watching the muscles contract at his touch. Before the exploration could follow that tempting treasure trail, Eric said, "My turn, babe. I need to taste you." He held Brad by his hips and lifted his body further up onto Eric's chest until the head of Brad's cock bumped against those soft lips.

Without saying another word, the tip of Eric's tongue slid out to taste the bead of cum on the head before swallowing him down his throat.

"Fuck, yeah," Brad yelled as the wet heat engulfed him.

Eric's tongue explored every inch of him, and Brad closed his eyes to get lost in unparalleled pleasure. Eric eased away from Brad's cock, and slowly Brad opened his eyes as something was placed in his hand. He looked down to find a small bottle of lube, and didn't have to guess what Eric wanted him to do.

While his lover resumed lavishing him with attention, Brad prepared himself. Using the lube, he first slipped one finger in slowly until he'd stretched himself enough to accommodate a second finger and then a third. Between the pleasure he was receiving, and giving to himself, he moaned and flexed his hips.

Eric released Brad's cock, twisted to reach beneath the mattress, and handed him a condom. "Put this on me, babe. I can't wait any longer to be inside you."

He hissed as Brad rolled down the latex, then gave Eric a couple of firm strokes. He grabbed the back of Brad's thighs and squeezed, encouraging Brad to get to his knees. "Put me inside you, Bradley." Eric's voice was rough and deep as if he were holding onto his control by his fingertips.

Brad reached down between his legs, lined up Eric's magnificent cock, and slowly lowered himself down, until he'd impaled himself on Eric. The moment his ass cheeks touched skin, Brad rose and slowly and did it again. And then, again.

Soon they found their rhythm, never once losing eye contact with one another. The intensity of their connection surprised Brad, considering this was the first time they'd had sex, but he didn't shy away from it. He embraced it, gathering it close, never wanting to forget this feeling.

Their pace increased, and Brad was getting close to coming. Eric shifted his hips slightly so that he was pegging Brad's prostate with every stroke.

"Going to blow," Brad huffed out.

Instead of slowing down, Eric bucked into Brad while taking hold of his cock and began pumping at the same speed as his thrusts. Fire raced down his spine, into his balls, and up his hard dick as he exploded on Eric's chest.

For a moment of sweet bliss, everything stopped as the rush of his orgasm took hold. The deep, thundering groan that registered in Brad's brain accompanied his lover's release, and he lowered the top of his body down onto Eric's chest, the stickiness gluing them together.

Brad's racing heartbeat matched his lover's while they gasped for air.

Chapter Ten

Eric watched the sky begin to lighten as he brought the blankets up over the top of the two of them before pulling Brad against his chest. Brad's disheveled curly blond hair obscured most of his face, but by the sounds of his continued snores, he was still asleep.

They'd stayed awake most of the night, unable to keep their hands off one another, dozing between bouts of incredible fucking. Eric had had more sex in one evening then he'd had in the last six months. Though, to be honest, somewhere around the third time, the fucking turned tender, and somehow emotions came into play.

Eric felt he'd given a part of himself to Brad somewhere, and didn't want it back. What they'd shared would leave a lasting effect on him, and Eric hoped his lover as well.

He ran the tips of his fingers through those soft curls, the thick strands catching on his calloused hands. He wondered how Brad had gotten so deep under his skin after only knowing each other a few months. Now he couldn't imagine a life without the man in it. He'd fallen fast and hard but had no desire to slow down.

This, right here, was what he'd been searching for.

A sense of calm filled him with peace as he closed his eyes and drifted back to sleep.

***

When he woke again, he found Brad laying on top of him, his chin resting on his hands looking down at Eric.

"Morning."

"Morning," Eric replied before leaning forward for a kiss. Brad didn't hesitate to close the distance between them. A small moan escaped his lover's lips, and he dove in for more, deepening the kiss.

When the kiss slowed, Eric pulled away and looked deeply into those gorgeous hazel eyes. "Now, this is the way to wake up."

"Seriously, I was thinking the same thing," Brad chuckled. "Not to rush things. And I'm fine with whatever you answer, but I've gotta ask, are we a couple? Like exclusive?"

Leave it to Brad to get to the heart of the matter right away. No need to let it percolate under the surface. He tilted his head, waiting for Eric's answer.

Eric wrapped his arms around Brad's waist and answered right away. "Yes. If that's what you want."

"I wouldn't've asked if I didn't want it." Brad grinned.

"Smartass. Do you have any plans for today?" He remembered Brad mentioning he had Sunday off.

"Nope," Brad answered. "Other than hanging out with Grams. It's Sunday, and if I'm not working, it's family day."

"Perfect. Since it's family day, I have an idea." Eric buzzed with excitement. "I have a reasonably sized backyard with a patio, and a new grill to break in. Why don't we have a barbeque here and bring your Grams out for the day? We could invite a few friends. What do you think?" Eric couldn't remember the last time he'd had a get-together at his place. It was time to fix that.

"We're making couples plans already," Brad joked. "I like the way you think, captain."

"Why waste time? Who would you like to invite?" he asked. Eric had always been a full speed kind of guy. Given his profession, he better than most knew life was short. When you knew something was right, why wait?

"I was thinking of the crew from The Gates. Saint, Max, Marian, Finn, Miguel, James, Ross, Sam, and Joey. I know some of them have to work, but we can extend the invite and see who's available and wants to come."

"Sounds great. I'll invite my landlady, Mrs. Alverez. She doesn't get out much anymore, so this might be a chance for her to have some fun," Eric suggested. "I think she and your grandmother would get along." His landlady had always been friendly, even dropping off the odd meal when he'd come home from the station.

"Now, I'm getting excited."

Eric couldn't help himself. He rubbed his semi-hard cock against Brad's thigh. "I'm getting excited as well."

He laughed and hugged Eric. "Your mouth or mine?"

"You choose."

Brad's eyebrows shot up, and he said with a sexy grin, "I want to taste you."

"Any time you want."

As Eric had learned last night, Bradley had a talented mouth, and as Eric cocked his legs, Brad slid down, cupped Eric's balls and sucked the head of his cock into welcome warmth.

After Eric had jerked off Bradley to a spectacular completion, they lay in each other's arms and Brad was quiet. Too quiet.

"What's wrong, Bradley?" When Eric didn't get an answer, he shook Brad, knowing he'd understand the physical hint to spit it out.

"I want you to know the truth about me," Brad muttered into Eric's chest.

"Only if you're ready." There was no way he would pressure him. Eric had no doubts about Brad's character.

Brad nodded. Then said nothing. After he took a deep breath, he pulled back a little and said, "I've already told you about my parents taking off when I was born and how Grams and Gramps took me in and raised me. I definitely wouldn't be here today if it weren't for them. They never treated me like a burden. They loved me as if I were their son."

"They're all that's good in society," Eric said. "I wish I could have met your Gramps."

"He would have liked you right from the start," Brad stated with conviction.

"Thank you." Eric considered that high praise.

"When Gramps became sick, it took a bit of fighting to get him to go in for a checkup. By the time he saw the doctor, his lung cancer had already reached stage two in his right lung. We were told he'd have to undergo radiation and chemotherapy to reduce the size of the lesions before they could operate. Of course, my Gramps took it like the strong man he was, determined he could beat it. I was in my final year of college, full scholarship at CalPoly Pomona in Applied Math and Robotics. I didn't finish."

Well shit. Eric knew Brad was smart and talented—no one could break into the security systems Brad had without serious skills. "I'm sorry about your Gramps and that you had to leave school."

Brad nodded. "One night, after the treatments had started, I overheard my grandparents talking in the kitchen. They were discussing the shop and all the medical bills that were starting to pile up. His cancer wasn't responding to the therapy, and the doctors wanted to add a new medication to his already lengthy list, but the cost would take what little savings they had left."

Eric knew where this was going, but he let Brad continue.

"I'd already taken over at the shop, but there was never enough money to cover all the bills, and creditors were beginning to harass them. One even came into the shop demanding money on the spot. I was able to get him to leave when I threatened to call the police. We closed the shop soon after."

Eric shifted their bodies until he had Brad tucked against his side with his head on Eric's chest. The need to comfort him was overpowering.

"I've always excelled in anything involving electronics and puzzles. It came naturally. I'd spent my childhood tearing things apart to see how they worked. A couple of people in the neighborhood knew what my family was going through, and one day I was approached with not your typical job offer, but one that…ah, appealed to my abilities."

Eric pulled him closer.

"Breaking into security systems was fairly easy. In my mind, they became puzzles to solve. I agreed on one condition. That we stole only from other criminals. There was no way I was going to steal from people who'd truly earned what they had. To the other guy, I was his golden goose. The money, as I'd hoped, soon became an answer to my prayers. We could afford Gramps's medications and therapies. Of course, by then, he was spending more time in the hospital than out. He never knew what I'd done to get the money."

It was apparent to Eric that Grams knew the truth by the way she'd spoken to him the day before about Brad's past. As if he'd heard Eric's thoughts, Brad carried on with his story.

"Grams knew, of course. I couldn't hide it from her. I tried to stop a couple of times, but then something would come up, and we'd need more money for his care, so I went back to it. Once Gramps's funeral was paid for, I planned to stop for good. Helping get Joey back was the first time I'd used those particular talents for something other than money. When I got shot and outted, I was no longer useful, which suited me fine. I wanted out, but that's not the kind of job you turn in a two-week notice and walk away."

Eric grunted at the absolute truth of that statement.

"I often wonder how disappointed Gramps would have been if he knew the truth."

Since his grandmother's love never wavered, it seems unlikely his grandfather would've been angry or disappointed in anything other than him having put Bradley in the position to have done what he did. Brad had done whatever he had to. Motivated by love and a lack of money to save his grandfather didn't legally forgive his adopted profession, but it explained it. The medical system could be vicious to those without insurance and the ability to pay.

"I believe your Gramps wouldn't have held that against you because of the position you and your Grams were in. Though I don't believe he'd've been happy you put yourself at risk like that, he would've understood. I'm sure of that." Eric gave Bradley a tight hug. "As you know, I'm not one to condone criminal acts, but I understand how things happen in extreme circumstances," Eric explained. "You're not a bad person. Not by a long shot."

Brad didn't respond, and Eric held him.

He'd been right when he believed Brad was a good person. He couldn't bury that part of himself. His heart was far too big to hide.

Eric couldn't imagine the strength it took for Brad to walk into a police station and admit he was a master thief who wanted to help his friend. Especially since he was living a double life. Trying to get out from under while aiming to build a life doing it legally.

The more Eric knew about Brad, the more he respected him, and the deeper he fell.

***

Freshly showered and shaved, Brad stood in his clothing from last night as he waited for Eric to get off the phone. He'd already confirmed with Saint that he, Max, and Marian would be coming to their barbeque, but Finn and Miguel would be on duty at The Gates. Grams almost screamed into the phone that she'd be coming as soon as they picked her up. Eric was on the phone with Detective Ross, and confirmed that Sam and Joey would be dropping by, along with a rookie police officer by the name of Clay.

"Okay, we'll see you then," Eric said before disconnecting the call and looking over at him. "Ross and James are in, and they're bringing Ross's sister and niece along."

"Sounds like we're having a real Sunday barbeque with family and friends," Brad said. "It's almost like a dream or some sort of seventies sitcom."

"I'm going with *'Happy Days.'*" Eric laughed.

"Why *'Happy Days'*?"

Eric raised his thumbs in front of him, struck a pose, and said, "Aaay."

"Oh my god, you're such a goof." Brad laughed. "I would never have guessed that from the big, bad, captain, I met a couple of months ago."

Eric walked over and took Brad into his arms. "There is a lot about me that only a few people get to see. I like to keep my professional and private lives separate."

"I can understand that," Brad agreed. "Hey, I've always wondered why you hadn't arrested me when I came to the station to help with Joey's rescue. I flat-out admitted what I'd done."

"It's a complicated legal thing," Eric joked while holding him close. "Proof." Brad's head jerked back. "You can say whatever you want, but without any proof or police reports substantiating a house was burgled, on what ground was I going to arrest you? You said you were a cat burglar, not what and who you stole from. When you said criminals don't call the cops when something goes missing, you were right."

"Did you check to see if there were reports filed after we rescued Joey?"

"Sure I did."

Brad wrapped his arms around his neck and said, "I would have expected nothing less from my captain. I respect that." He looked into Eric's eyes. "Truth. Has it been difficult being out on the police force?"

"Not as difficult as having a homophobic stepfather," Eric shared, his expression turning dour.

"That sucks. Does your mom feel the same way?"

"She doesn't know I'm gay."

Those words thundered through Brad's mind as warning bells began sounding. Eric wasn't out to his family, and that only meant one thing.

Brad stepped out of their embrace and said, "I won't be someone's dirty secret. Not even for you." Though it would hurt him to let the captain go, he'd already spent too many years in the shadows. He wasn't willing to step back into them again."

Eric moved forward and took hold of both of Brad's hands. "I would never ask you to be my secret. I'm proud we're together, and I don't give a damn who knows it. I'll tell her."

"Why haven't you already?" That was a lot of years in hiding and had to make for tense-as-shit family visits.

"I wanted to, but I went to my stepfather, Dan, first. What did I know? I was only a dumb teenager trying to figure out all these strange feelings." Eric led Brad over to the couch where they both sat down.

"It didn't go well?" Brad asked.

"That's an understatement. He slapped me across my face and told me that no stepson of his was coming out as gay. If I tried, he'd leave my mom with nothing."

"Holy fuck," Brad growled. "What an asshole. That is *so* wrong."

"Yeah. So, you can imagine I kept that part of me to myself. When I was out of school and the academy, I made sure I got a job far away from them so I could live my life, but I could support my mom if the asshole left her when I came out."

"What happened?"

"My mom started having problems with her blood pressure and heart. She's on medication, and has been to a few cardiologists about her arrhythmia, but so far no one has been able to get it under control. Next week, she's going to another cardiologist, and we'll see what she says."

"You were worried about her health, so you didn't tell her?" Brad moved closer to his side.

Eric nodded. "Especially after Dan said shock might be enough to stress her weak heart."

"Have you tried to tell her by hints? You know, not all at once."

"I don't even know where to begin now, and every time I try, Dan shows up. It's like he has some sort of sixth sense about it. At times I wonder if he's truly concerned about her health, or if he's become used to his life of leisure."

"Leisure?"

"Since they've retired, I've been sending Dan extra money every month to care for her, and any added expenses that might come up.

My mom needs it, but I worry how much of it she's receiving. I don't trust him, but she seems happy, so I'm caught between doing what feels right, which is cutting off the money since he's the one handling it, and doing what she needs."

Brad couldn't be upset at Eric about this. By the look on his face, he was already beating himself up about it. "We'll figure this all out together."

Eric scanned Brad's face as if searching for duplicity, and Brad figured Eric had decided Brad was telling the truth when Eric pulled him in for a tight hug.

"Thank you for understanding." Eric gave him a quick kiss. "I don't want you to feel like I'm keeping you a secret. Ever."

"Well, considering we're hosting a barbeque, I think we're past that point with our friends."

"Damn right," Eric said. "Am I moving too fast? I don't want to pressure you into anything or bulldoze you."

Instead of answering right away, Brad shifted closer until he was leaning against Eric's chest. "For the first time, I'm going after what I want. I'm not about to hold back."

Eric's smile was all the response Brad required. He took Eric's chin in his hand, and went in for a deep kiss that had him gasping when they broke apart.

"Okay, then. We are both on the same page," Eric rasped. "Hey, do you have a valid driver's license?"

He found that random but answered, "Yeah. Gramps used to have a car. I drove Grams around until it rusted off its frame. Why?"

"I thought while I waited here for the groceries to be delivered, you could take the truck to go home to change and pick up Grams. Maybe pack a few things to keep here if you want."

Brad had to wonder if the shock was written all over his face. Keep some clothes at Eric's house? Talk about moving at the speed of light. Plus, Eric babied that truck and was going to hand the keys to him. WTF?

Brad tilted his head back to look Eric in the eye. "Are you sure?"

"Yep. While you're gone, I'll get started on the food." Eric gave Brad a squeeze. They parted and Eric grabbed his keys from a hook in the kitchen and slid one off the ring before handing it to Brad.

"Be careful," Eric said.

"I promise I won't get a scratch on it." Maybe he should take the bus.

Eric's brows furrowed and he shook his head, confusing Brad. "No, I'm not worried about the truck. I don't want you or Grams to get into an accident. There are some crazy-ass drivers out there. I've seen what can happen. Trucks are replaceable. You two aren't."

That warm feeling settled in Brad's chest. Eric was worried about their safety, not his truck, and Brad knew the captain loved his truck. The feel of being treasured was intoxicating.

Brad moved to the door with the key in hand. "Totally careful. I'll be back soon."

Eric leaned down for a kiss, which Brad was more than eager to give, before heading for the side door. The big guy didn't follow him. Instead, he was pulling bowls out of the cupboards. He wasn't even going to check if Brad could get out of the driveway or watch him drive away.

So much had changed in these past few months. It had all started when he'd taken a bartending position at The Gates. Maybe that old building had some sort of magic.

The Gates had changed his life, definitely for the better.

Chapter Eleven

The backyard echoed with conversation and laughter, leaving Brad with the unusual sense of belonging. The groceries had arrived while he was gone, and Eric had gotten busy with preparations.

They made a huge garden salad with sides of grilled zucchini, three-bean dip, guacamole and chips. Mrs. Alverez made tacos, with Marian's assistance, while Grams made her legendary chiffon cake.

Eric lorded over his grill, and Brad found it endearing. Hamburgers, brats, and grilled corn on the cob filled the air with that unmistakable barbeque aroma.

There were bottles of California white wine, 805 beer, juice, and bottled water sitting in an ice-filled tub against the side fence. The red wine was on the table under the patio overhang, where the food was laid out. Lawn chairs and the chairs to the outdoor table were scattered around landscaping that was a mix of succulents, stone walkways and seagrass, much like the front of the house, neat and tidy.

Grams, Marian, and Mrs. Alverez, had hit it off immediately, and the three sat back in loungers under a shady umbrella deep in conversation. Grams hadn't stopped talking from the time he'd gotten her picked up to now.

If she'd had her way, Eric would be up for sainthood. No matter how many times Brad reminded her that it was early days in their relationship and anything could happen, Grams wasn't buying it. She touched the side of her nose and said, "I know what I know, and that man's a keeper."

Brad had always been fiercely independent and somewhat fearless to the point of stupidity—cat burglar. The thought of being attached to another person had its attraction, but Brad wasn't certain he knew how to navigate the whole relationship thing. As if Eric knew his thoughts, he turned from the grill, caught Brad's eye and smiled.

For most of the afternoon, Eric, Ross, and James stood around the grill, beers in hand laughing. Ross's sister, Jac, and her daughter, Becca, had come, and Jac was busy fussing with the food, making sure bowls were filled, and condiments were plenty. Becca was playing with Mrs. Alverez's golden retriever, Buddy. Every so often, a yellow tennis ball would land in the midst of the group, followed by an excited dog.

Joey, Sam, and their guest, Clay, hadn't arrived yet but were on their way. Everything seemed to be perfect, which worried Brad. In his world, when things were going too well, the other shoe fell and shit happened.

"Why so worried?" Jac asked, surprising him.

"I'm not worried," Brad said. She arched a brow. He threw his hand out. "Too good."

"Ah. The 'something bad has to happen' phase." She nodded.

"Yeah." Brad ran the palm of his hand down his face.

"I'd gone through something similar after my husband died," she shared.

"Oh, god. I'm sorry." That explained why he wasn't here with them. Brad felt sad for Becca not knowing her father. He could relate.

"Don't be. He wasn't all that he seemed when I married him. He almost cost Becca, Ross, James, and me our lives," she near snarled then waved her hand. "Back to you. After everything settled down, and life was good again, I began experiencing bouts of paralyzing fear. I convinced myself the happiness wouldn't last, but it did."

"When did you stop worrying?" Brad hoped it was sooner rather than later.

"You don't. Not really," she said, dashing his hopes. "But over time, the fear will grow smaller until it's only an occasional thought that vanishes as quickly as it came."

Brad looked over at her and said, "I hope you're right. I'd like to see where this goes."

"By the way that man looks at you, I don't think you need to worry overly much," she said with a wink.

He glanced back toward the grill, locking eyes with the man he'd come to care about over the past few months.

It was time for him to check in on the protein portion of this barbeque. He strode across the yard and up to Eric's side. The captain wrapped his free arm around Brad's waist.

"Everything is ready and set out," Brad said. "How's the meat coming along?"

Eric leaned down and kissed his temple, and surprisingly no one batted an eye. The conversation carried on, burgers flipped, and Buddy came barreling through chasing after his ball. It felt normal, how life should be.

Before Eric had a chance to answer, Joey, Sam, and a third man came walking into the backyard through the fence gate. The stranger had short brown hair and was about the same height as Sam, less muscled, but toned. This new arrival had to be the rookie Eric had told him about.

"Hey guys," James said. "Bout time you showed up, we were about to eat without you."

All three smiled. "Yeah, yeah, yeah. Paperwork to finish up," Sam explained. "Blame my captain." Eric smiled wide.

Joey was carrying a tray covered with aluminum foil. "What'd you bring?" Brad asked.

"Chile relleno," he said. "My mom used to love spicy foods."

"Sounds perfect," Brad agreed. "Bring on the heat."

"Bradley, I'd like to introduce you to Clay Everett," Eric said while still holding him close. "He's new to our unit."

Brad held out his hand to shake Clay's, and the rookie said, "So, you're the thief."

The yard fell silent.

When it appeared as though Eric was about to speak, Brad stopped him with a squeeze.

"Yeah, that's me."

Then Clay did something Brad hadn't expected. He took Brad's hand and shook it. "It's an honor to meet you. I've heard you took a bullet protecting two officers. You're a hero."

Not what Brad was expecting, and he got tongue-tied for a moment.

"Yep, he's a hero," Eric said. "He pushed me and Sam out of the way when we stormed the house where Joey was held. Who knows what would have happened if he hadn't." Eric pulled Brad closer and kissed the side of his head. "You could say he's my guardian angel."

"You'll have to tell me the story sometime," Clay said, before taking the plate from Joey. "I'll go set this on the table with the other fixings for you."

"Thank you," Joey responded and smiled. "That's kind of you."

Brad swore he saw the man's cheeks brighten at the compliment.

Once Clay was out of earshot, he had to ask, "That's the problem rookie you told me about?" he whispered in Eric's ear.

"That's the one," Eric whispered back. "Though I'm beginning to wonder about those reports."

"Hey," Sam said. "I have to admit when I invited him to come along, considering he starts on Monday, I had a few concerns. However, he's been friendly and asking questions. Nothing to indicate he's a problem."

"I was surprised he agreed to join us considering he doesn't know any of us except Sam and Eric, and even then, it was only for a quick meeting," Ross said. "A bit more investigation might be in order."

"You're off the clock, detective," James protested. "Leave it for another day."

"Well, it looks like you guys were worried for nothing." Joey summed it up. "I have to admit it makes me wonder what really happened."

Joey reached out and took Brad's hand, said, "show me around," and changed the subject.

Brad looked up at Eric who smiled and titled his head toward the house. "Have at it." Then he kissed him.

The two walked in the house, and the moment they cleared the doorway, Joey was on him. "That must have been one hell of a date."

Brad couldn't help but laugh. He pulled two bottles of water out of the fridge and handed one to Joey. "You could say that. Do you want to sit down?" Joey's strength wasn't always a given, and he wasn't a complainer. More often than not, he toughed it out when he didn't have to.

"Sure, I didn't want a tour anyways," he admitted. "I wanted time to talk with you. So, tell me. What happened? A little over a month ago, you didn't know if you wanted to accept his ride to PT. Now, you're playing house." His mischievous grin accompanied the sparkle in his eyes.

"I don't have a clue," Brad admitted. "The more we got to know each other, the more we clicked. The incident at the convenience store seemed to hit home for both of us. You know, life's short, don't waste it. Yesterday, we had the best time. Fun and easy. One thing led to another, and here we are."

"That man looks at you like he could eat you up," Joey said. "I knew something was going on between the two of you these last couple weeks. You weren't put out about spending time with Eric anymore. You seemed to be looking forward to it even."

"I didn't even realize," Brad said. "It sort of fell into place."

"That's the best way, when you don't have to push it to make it happen. You came together naturally."

"Was that what happened between you and Sam?"

"Yes. From the first moment I saw him, I felt it, but then again, I fought it long enough. I should listen to my advice sometimes." Joey huffed before taking a drink from his water bottle. "All's well that ends well, or so they say." His smile was wide, assuring Brad that he genuinely was happy.

The two sat for another thirty minutes, talking before Sam stuck his head in the door and yelled, "Food's on." The burgers and brats were cooked perfectly, the tacos and chile relleno went like wildfire, and the side dishes vanished faster than Brad could have guessed they would. These men ate like food was going out of style.

They spent the rest of the afternoon talking, drinking, and lounging in the backyard as evening set in, and the sky turned SoCal pink as the sun set to the west over the Pacific. When Brad looked around at all the people he cared about, and his new friends, he couldn't help but think of his Gramps and how much he would have enjoyed today.

I think I've found my place, Gramps.

Chapter Twelve

Two weeks later

Eric looked down at the sleeping man in his arms. They'd stayed up late to watch an action movie marathon, and Brad had fallen asleep half an hour ago, with his head on Eric's lap. He ran his fingers through Brad's golden hair and thought about the last few weeks, which had been some of the happiest in his life.

Brad had been spending more and more time over at his house now that he didn't have to worry about leaving Grams alone. She and Mrs. Alverez had hit it off so well that when Brad came over to Eric's, Grams visited with Eric's landlady. They were both elderly widows, and Eric hadn't seen Mrs. Alverez this active in years. A definite win-win.

Although he'd lived in this house for years, he'd never felt as at home here as he did now. His world was filled with life and laughter, as well as things he hadn't realized he'd been missing, like community and friendship. Eric had spent most of his time consumed with proving he was worthy of being a captain, especially at his younger age, and he'd missed out on a life away from policing.

He swore he'd never go back to the way things were. He couldn't. He was in love with this beautiful man who had changed his life so profoundly. For once, he was looking forward to his birthday tomorrow.

The reflection of headlights tracked across his living room wall, and Eric looked at his watch. It was after eleven in the evening. Who would be stopping in at this time of night? Then he remembered Grams and Mrs. Alverez liked to order takeout late at night. They behaved like teenagers, and Eric thought it was great to see.

He went back to watching the movie while keeping an ear out for the delivery driver. His and his landlady's house were close enough that he could hear when someone came to her door. What he wasn't expecting was the key sliding into the lock of his side door instead.

Quickly, Eric woke his disoriented lover before standing to meet whoever it was at his door before they could get too far inside his home. He made it halfway across the room when the door opened, revealing his stepfather and mother.

"Dan. Mom. What are you guys doing here?" he asked in a slightly higher tone of voice than usual.

"We wanted to surprise you for your birthday, sweetheart." His mom said before walking up to him and giving him a big hug.

Dan brought their luggage in and sat it by the door while his mom fussed. He knew the moment his stepfather caught sight of Brad, and Dan's expression went from annoyed to enraged. That one vein that typically popped out on his forehead when he was angry blew up like a balloon.

"Oh, who do we have here?" Mom asked, her tone as cheerful as ever.

Eric turned and went to stand beside Brad placing his arm around his lover's back. He wouldn't deny who Brad was to him.

"This is Bradley," Eric said. "My boyfriend."

Without missing a beat, his mom stepped forward and gave Brad a considerable hug, confusing Eric.

"Finally, I get to meet one. I thought you'd never bring a nice boy home for me to gush over." She appeared to be relieved, not angry or upset.

Eric and Brad looked at each other, equally confused. However, neither had the time to deal as Dan eyed Brad before he took a step toward them. Eric quickly moved his mom and Brad behind him moments before Dan delivered a mean uppercut across his jaw.

He saw stars for a few seconds, and he swore his teeth rattled, but he didn't move a muscle.

"Oh my God, Dan. What have you done?" Mom asked, and Eric turned slightly to find her in Brad's arms. It relieved him to know she was in good hands.

"Fucking faggot," Dan sneered. "I warned you to keep that disgraceful behavior in your fucking pants."

"What?" Mom growled. Janet Meyers was not a woman to be messed with. She'd been a single mother, and it had been the two of them for a long time. She was as tough as they came, until her health began declining.

"Mom, please calm down. Your heart can't take it," Eric begged. "Bradley, can you take her to the spare bedroom and make up the bed while I deal with this."

"Of course," Brad answered, but his mom wouldn't move.

"My heart?" she asked. "My heart is fine, never better. It's been years since I've had any spikes in my blood pressure. I keep telling you that."

Eric wasn't sure he understood this right. Was she trying to downplay her illness again?

"I don't understand. Dan told me you were on heavy doses of medications and seeing a cardiologist. That any shock could cause you to have a heart attack."

She looked over at Dan, her eyes wide as saucers. "You lied to him," she hissed. "Why?"

Dan still looked ready to blow. "I had to keep this embarrassment in line somehow."

"Embarrassment," Eric growled. "You weren't embarrassed when you took my money to pay the bills, even after I paid off your mortgage."

"I think I need to sit down," Mom said. When he held her elbow and tried to help lower her to the sofa, she chastised him. "I'm not having a heart attack. Stop fussin'."

Eric raised his hands in surrender. He was watchful to keep his body between his mom, Bradley, and Dan. He didn't trust the man who had assaulted and battered an LAPD captain in his home. Eric would hang onto that nugget for a minute. Now that the dirty secrets were coming to light, Dan didn't seem quite so cocky.

"We should go," Dan spat out. "Get your things, Janet."

"Shut up," she replied. "If you want to go, then go."

Dan stepped back as if she'd struck him. "How dare you talk to me like that?"

Before he had a chance to move closer, Eric stepped in his way. "Try it. You had one freebee, old man. The next move you make determines whether I arrest you for hitting an officer of the law."

"Just go, Dan. I'll stay here with my son. You can stay in a hotel if you want until I get to the bottom of this." His mother waved her hands in the air stressing the "this."

"What the hell do you think you're doing?" Dan bellowed. "Get up this instant."

"I'm doing something I should have done long ago—listen to what my son is trying to tell me. Now leave." She turned away from Dan to face her son. "I'm so sorry, Eric."

The bastard took that one step closer, causing Eric to puff out his chest and growl, "Get out of my house before I arrest you."

"You wouldn't dare." The idiot tried to puff out his chest and Eric almost laughed. "You forget I used to be a police captain in this city. I've got friends in places you don't even know about. I could make your life hell."

"Try me." Eric didn't feel threatened in the slightest. He'd done a little digging years ago, and he doubted Dan had as many friends as he thought he had. The man had burned a lot of bridges over his career. It wasn't hard for Eric to see why.

"Hell, I'll take a picture while you cuff him, babe," Brad added. "You want to keep that shit for posterity. Have it blown up into a poster."

Eric couldn't help it. This time he laughed. Leave it to his love to put the perfect dig into the situation.

"Just go, Dan. We'll talk tomorrow." His mom looked tired all of a sudden, and Eric knew he'd caused that.

"Fine, stay here with these freaks." Dan stormed to the door, picked up one of the suitcases, and looked back at Eric. "This isn't over."

"It is for me," Eric growled. "You're no longer in control, and you are not welcome in this house. Don't come back here."

In Dan's anger, he forcefully pulled the door open, slamming the handle into the drywall, leaving a circular hole behind. Eric looked out to find Grams and Mrs. Alverez standing in their doorway, obviously having heard the commotion. Buddy barked from somewhere behind them.

Mrs. Alverez clung to her phone and asked. "Do you want me to call the police, Eric?"

Dan huffed in disgust. "What the hell kind of fucked-up shit is all this? The gay granny brigade?"

Grams lifted a .38 special she'd been holding behind her robe, pointed at the ground in front of Dan, and said, "You got a problem with that?" *Holy shit.*

Dan seemed as surprised as Eric, and wisely bee-lined it for his rental. With the squeal of car tires as he peeled out, the asshole was gone. At least for now.

"Is everything all right?" Mrs. Alverez asked, her one hand hovering above her heart.

"Yes, thank you, ladies. My stepfather shouldn't be any more of a problem. I'm sorry we woke you."

"Don't worry about waking us. We're waiting on our pizza anyway," Grams said as she returned the gun to a lockbox that Eric hadn't noticed sitting on the bench of her walker. Well, at least she stored it properly.

"We'll talk in the morning. Goodnight, ladies." He had to get back to his mother to make sure she was okay.

"Goodnight," they responded in unison.

Eric shut and relocked the door before turning to find his mother standing only a couple of feet away from him. She opened her arms, and Eric gladly filled them. Behind her, he could see Brad still sitting on the couch, tears in his eyes and a crooked smile on his face. His words from weeks ago echoed in Eric's head.

We'll figure this out together.

***

Brad wasn't sure if he should stay or go to give them some privacy to talk. He sat on the couch and watched as the two hugged. Their nice quiet evening of mindless action movies had exploded into a full-blown assault, battery, and threats, the trifecta of family dysfunction. Maybe he should go.

Standing, he gathered his apartment keys, wallet, and cellphone before putting on his shoes. Brad hoped Mrs. Alverez wouldn't mind him sleeping on her couch for the night. Eric needed time alone with his mother.

When he turned, Eric was right beside him. "You're leaving?"

"I thought I'd go next door so that you and your mom can have some time alone together to talk." He imagined they had a lot to discuss after what came to light tonight.

"You're coming back in the morning?" His concern was evident.

Brad finally realized how bad this looked to Eric and wrapped his arms around the big guy's neck. His injured left arm pulled slightly, but there was no pain. "Definitely. Nothing could keep me away from you."

Eric's face softened, and he smiled. "I'll hold you to that."

"You'd better." Brad wiggled his brows for good measure as he looked up into Eric's handsome face.

They kissed briefly, no need to shock his mother any more than she already was. Eric took hold of his hand, and they headed to the door.

"Oh no. You're not leaving because of what happened?" she asked as she headed them off from making it to the door. "Please don't leave my son because of this. He's a good man."

Brad took hold of her hand and said, "He certainly is. I'll come back tomorrow. The two of you need time to talk without me here. It was nice meeting you, Janet."

She squeezed his hand before letting it go. "Then, we will get to know each other better tomorrow."

He nodded his agreement, opened the door, and kissed Eric one more time. When he shut the door behind him, the sounds of the city comforted him.

One constant was this city. Los Angeles may change and grow with the times, but the City of Angels never stopped, and neither would he.

He was prepared to fight for the life he'd found.

***

His fist hovered in front of the door. Brad had asked Grams and Mrs. Alverez to wait before coming over because he wasn't sure what he was walking into. He'd waited for a decent time in the morning to come back over, but now he wasn't sure if he should knock.

While he debated, the door opened, revealing Eric, who appeared to be coming outside. His eyes widened when he saw Brad.

"I was coming over to you," he said.

"I was coming over to you," Brad responded before Eric pulled him against his chest.

As he snuggled closer, he realized that Eric had been as worried as he was about this morning.

"Coffee?" Eric asked.

"No," he replied, and at the captain's look of concern, he continued. "Kiss first, coffee second."

He broke out into a smile, and his eyes softened. "I accept your terms."

His soft lips lowered and covered Brad's, and a kiss that began innocently enough turned heated as their tongues explored. Brad's body soon began to react to the sexy man in his arms when he heard the door behind them click open.

"I see you've found your man, perfect." Janet's voice was cheerful, and a bit relieved, he thought. "Bring him inside so I can feed him."

Eric slowed the kiss, and Brad's heated thoughts cooled instantly, taking the apparent signs of his excitement with them. Caught by your boyfriend's mother. He could say he'd never expected to say that at his age.

Brad's laughter came out of nowhere at the thought that, less than twelve hours ago, he was sleeping happily with his head on his boyfriend's lap.

Eric joined with his laughter while Janet shook her head at the two of them. "You're both goofballs."

"We'll be in in a moment, Mom."

She smiled much like her son, full of happiness, and shut the door.

"By the look on your mother's face, I'm taking it that your discussion went well?" Brad asked.

"It did. We stayed up for hours, and I told her everything that happened since I first went to Dan for advice. My mother didn't know anything about what was going on. The money, the lies about her health, the way Dan made it seem she'd be upset if I came out as gay even though she'd already suspected I was. The times I'd asked her about her blood pressure, she was telling me the truth when she said she was fine. Dan had convinced me it was because she didn't want me to worry. I can't believe I fell for it. Some police captain I turned out to be."

Brad would not allow Eric to disparage himself. "When it comes to family, it's completely different than what you have to deal with in your career. Don't go talking shit about the man I love."

The words were out of Brad's mouth before he even realized what he was saying. Of course, he'd thought about the fact that he'd fallen in love with Eric over the past weeks, but he hadn't intended to say so until they had more time in to work out the newness of their relationship. Would this scare Eric off?

One moment he was standing on the ground; the next, he was spinning around in the air in Eric's arms. When the captain slowed, he looked at Brad as if he'd won some sort of prize—shocked but happy.

"I love you, too, and I'm not saying that because you did first. I've been thinking and feeling it for a while now."

Brad didn't have the words, so he chose to show him exactly how he felt with a kiss. They loved each other. It was more than he'd ever dreamed possible, and Eric was his as much as he belonged to Eric.

"Happy birthday, love," Brad whispered when the kiss ended.

Chapter Thirteen

Eric had been over the report three times, and he still couldn't determine what about it was bothering him the most. The blatant violence involved or the targeted group. Both perspectives disgusted him.

Over the past eight days, there had been four separate attacks against members of the LGBTQ+ community. Every other day, like clockwork, he'd read a new report from around the city. Each had occurred outside gay bars and hotspots frequented by the community from West Hollywood to DTLA. No motive or connection, other than the fact that the victims were gay.

All signs led to one conclusion: they had a gay-basher on their hands. They had to find him or them fast before assault and battery turned into homicide. The chief had directed each area affected to assign members of their unit to a task force. Eric had three detectives working on the case, including Ross. The man had an uncanny ability to puzzle out even the most random of crimes. Eric had also increased patrols in the areas around known gay bars and clubs, hoping to catch whoever it was before they struck again.

He'd asked Brad to be even more alert on his walks from work to his apartment, and began rearranging his schedule to make sure he was available to give him a ride home. However, the plan wasn't perfect. Sometimes he couldn't make it, and those were the times he kept his phone close by in case Brad needed him.

His mother had called to let him know that some of her belongings would be delivered today. Good friends of hers who'd watched over the house when they were out of town had packed a few items up for her and shipped them by courier to Eric's house. She would be staying in his spare bedroom until she decided what she wanted to do. Considering she'd already been in touch with her lawyer, it seemed she had already made up her mind.

The odd thing about all of this was that Dan hadn't been seen or heard from since his mother told him she wanted a divorce. He hadn't returned to Florida, and Eric hadn't been able to find his name on the registry of any of the nearby hotels. Dan's rental car wasn't returned to the lot, and it still hadn't been found.

Sam and Ross agreed that Dan was most likely out on a tear. Boozing it up in Vegas or someplace not too far from LA, in an attempt to make Eric's mother worry about him. Eric thought of how angry and petulant Dan was on a good day, and agreed it was possible, but he would feel better once he knew for sure where Dan was hiding out.

A knock brought him out of his thoughts, and he looked up from his computer screen to find Clay standing outside his office.

"Come in," Eric said as he closed down the report and locked his computer. "Shut the door, please."

"You wanted to see me, Captain?" Clay asked.

"Yes. Have a seat."

"Okay," Clay said as his eyebrow furrowed. "What's wrong?"

"Nothing, I assure you. I wanted to check in with you since you've been here for a couple of weeks now. See how you're feeling everything is working out. Check if you need anything or have questions."

Clay looked a bit suspicious but answered anyway. "I believe that I fit in well. No one has mentioned anything to me."

"Me either, at least nothing disparaging. The other officers say you're top-notch. No complaints at all." It wasn't what Eric had expected after reading the file he was privy to prior to the transfer.

Clay seemed to calm at that statement as if he were expecting the opposite. Interesting. "You have to know what I'm wondering. You're intelligent, conscientious, thorough, and your work ethic is spot on. You came to me by way of a transfer after you were involved in an altercation with a fellow officer."

"Yes, sir. That is all true."

"Do you want to tell me what happened, or are you biding your time before doing something along the same lines here? I can guarantee you that if you do, it won't go well for you." Eric had always been direct. What was the use in easing into it? Facts were facts, and he'd tell it the way it was. It was his duty to watch over the officers under his command.

"I can understand your concern," Clay stated. "Looking at it from your point of view, I admit it does look odd. However, I can guarantee that nothing like that will ever happen here."

"I'm supposed to take your word for that?"

"No. However, considering you don't have a homophobic brother assigned to be my partner, I think the odds are in our favor."

"Are you saying that you were targeted due to your sexual orientation?" That shit wouldn't fly with Eric.

"It doesn't matter now. I'm here, I'm happy, and I can already feel the difference in the level of acceptance I've found."

"Is that why you locked your fellow officer in a PortaPotty?" Eric asked. "I remember your file mentioning something about locking him up with the shit he liked to stir up."

Clay smiled wide, not even trying to hide it. "That sounds about right again, sir. The officer in question began spreading rumors about me and even went as far as saying I made a pass at him."

"There wasn't a reprimand in your file. Why?"

"Technology. Considering the guy was the captain's brother, it wouldn't have been prudent to discipline me once I explained that I had tapped a few conversations between myself and the other officer. I think it might have been the one in which he swore to get my gay ass thrown off the force by any means possible that did it. Or it could have been the one when he threatened to use his brother, my former captain, to destroy my career."

Eric leaned back in his chair and looked at the rookie. "You could still file a grievance with the union."

Clay shook his head. "Not interested. I'm better off now and have no desire to relive it."

"I can respect that," Eric agreed. "However, if you ever change your mind, let me know."

Clay stood and reached out his hand. "Thank you, sir."

Eric also stood and shook Clay's hand. "You're welcome, and I swear you won't have to deal with any bullshit like that here."

He couldn't help but laugh when Clay used his own words against him.

"I'm supposed to take your word for that?"

Yep, he'd fit in fine.

***

Brad and Finn carried the garbage bags out to the Dumpster behind The Gates as they did after close every night. Finn managed the bar and restaurant for Saint and had been here since the beginning, before the building had begun to be renovated.

At the time, Finn had been homeless and living in the vestibule out in front of the empty building. Now, he and his boyfriend, Miguel, Max's right-hand man in his construction company, fed the homeless in Skid Row a couple of times a week. Most of the businesses in the surrounding blocks took part by donating food and supplies.

"So, still floating around on a cloud of love?" Finn teased while hoisting one bag over the top and into the bin.

"Not planning on landing for a good long while," Brad answered honestly.

"Good for you. I'm so happy to hear it," Finn said before tossing a second bag into the dumpster.

"How's your cat, Velcro, doing after her vet visit?" he asked. Finn loved the little hairball, and Brad was fond of her as well.

"By the time we got her home, pissed off was an understatement, but we had to get her spayed before she went into that heat madness again. I never want to hear her howl like that for as long as I live."

"Agreed." Brad had seen one such episode when he'd been invited over along with Joey.

Brad lifted another bag only to have it explode in his hands. He heard another gunshot and dove behind the Dumpster, taking Finn with him. Who the hell was shooting at him? *Again.* He'd had enough of this shit.

Brad looked back at Finn to find him on his cellphone, likely calling for help to someone in the building only a few yards away. They didn't dare try to make a run for the safety of The Gates. They didn't know exactly where the shooter was other than on the opposite side of the street.

"Help's on the way," Finn said as they both crouched as far behind the Dumpster as they could squeeze. "Why do people keep shooting at me?"

Brad looked over at him. "I was thinking the same thing except about me, not you. What does that say about us?"

"Maybe it's a random attack. There was news about gay men targeted around the city." Finn spoke calmly as if this sort of thing were commonplace.

He heard the sound of sirens getting closer to their location, and Brad hoped Eric was one of them since he was on duty tonight. Typically, captains didn't roll out on 911 calls, but Brad had a feeling if Eric knew a shooting was reported behind The Gates, Eric would be there. Brad could sure use a few minutes or more in those strong arms.

They hadn't heard any further shots, making Brad wonder if the shooter had taken off or was waiting them out. The back door of The Gates creaked opened slowly, and the tip of a rifle barrel peeked out only a few feet off the ground. Where the hell did they keep rifles in The Gates?

Miguel slowly inched out close to the ground and slid down the stairs. Finn's boyfriend was a retired Marine, but still worked the odd job for the government. Within seconds, he was in position behind one of Max's work trucks.

"We're okay," Finn said loud enough for Miguel to hear, and Brad watched as the big, tough guy seemed to calm almost immediately. "Who did you piss off, mister?"

Miguel shrugged his big shoulders, and Brad had to wonder if this had happened before. The Marine went on missions all over the world on behalf of the government, mostly on covert operations. Maybe this had nothing to do with Brad or the asshole staking out gay bars.

He turned back, and Miguel had vanished. Brad looked at Finn for answers.

"Don't worry. He's out there hunting the shooter. We're safest right here where he can protect us."

Brad was on board with that. He had no intention of moving until the flashing lights of squad cars appeared. How had taking out the garbage turned into a life-or-death decision? He wasn't ashamed to admit he needed his man, and he needed him now.

Squealing tires turning the corner, accompanied by flashing red and blue, alerted them to the arrival of the LAPD. Brad let out a deep breath in relief. Even though he desperately wanted to find Eric, Brad knew someone would come for them when it was safe. He and Finn stayed hunkered down side by side and waited.

Police cruisers sped up and down the streets, making Brad suspect they were still looking for the shooter. The sound of gravel crunching under boots had both of them huddling even closer. There was no way whoever it was who'd taken a shot at them made it through the police and Miguel.

Shadows appeared first from around the side of the Dumpster followed by the men they needed, Eric and Miguel. Brad jumped to his feet and ran into Eric's waiting arms.

"I've got you, love. You're safe," Eric repeated the statement over and over as Brad buried his face into the side of his neck.

A long night slinging drinks followed by a sneak attack shootout was enough for him. "I want to go home."

Eric grabbed Brad's hand and began walking. Fast. Brad kept his eyes on his feet while he kept pace with Eric's longer legs, not caring where they were going, as long as it was away from the Dumpster. A door closed behind them, and a few moments later the flooring registered, and he knew he was back inside The Gates. The next minute he was sitting on something soft.

He looked up to find himself in the hub at the back of The Gates where Saint, Max, and Marian lived until the condominiums were completed on the upper floors. The second level was already done, and Joey and Sam had bought the first unit.

"I can't take you home yet, Bradley, but I will as soon as the area is clear," Eric said as Marian came into the room.

"They need you outside," she said. "I'll sit with Brad until you come back."

She went over to the small kitchenette they'd set up in the hub for necessities when there was no kitchen, no bar, no nothing. Now that they were open for business, their meals could be made in the industrial kitchen used for serving the dining room of The Gates.

"I'll be back as soon as possible, I promise." Eric's dark eyes searched Brad's face and body as if looking for any injury.

"I'm fine. Really. Not a scratch. Go, do what you need to do," Brad said as he cupped the side of his lover's face. "I'll be right here."

"I love you," Eric said before quickly kissing Brad.

"I love you, too. Now go, find out who did this."

"I will," Eric said as he stood. "You have my word on that."

Brad watched him leave, the entire time wishing Eric didn't have to go back out and hunt down the person responsible for this shit. However, worried he was, Brad understood that this was Eric's job, his calling, and Brad respected that.

Chapter Fourteen

"Tell me someone picked this guy up?" Eric demanded as he joined the group assembled in the lot back behind The Gates. "We were here within four minutes of the call. He couldn't have gotten far."

"Not as of yet, sir," Sergeant Willows replied, her face rigid with anger.

"We have officers combing every street and alley in a ten-block radius," Ross said.

Eric walked over to the team securing the crime scene. He could see the twisted metal and hole in the side of the Dumpster. Two bags of garbage sat beside it, one sealed, and the other torn open with its contents lying over the pavement.

"What do you have for me?" he asked as he looked through the pissed-off expressions of the officers in the small group.

"Whoever made this shot wanted to do as much damage as possible. I won't know the caliber or make until I pull the slugs out of the concrete wall behind the Dumpster, but if I had to guess, with the size of the hole left behind, I would suspect a high-caliber rifle. Probably, a four-fifty-eight Winchester."

"Let me know when you have the answer."

"Yes, Captain."

Eric listened to a few of his officers checking in over their radios. Nothing. No sign of anything out of the ordinary. It was as if the person had vanished, which was impossible unless they had help.

He heard Sam's voice come across his radio with a report of an abandoned vehicle two blocks away. Something about it bothered Eric, so he responded, while Sam and Clay waited for him there.

"I'm going to check on that abandoned vehicle," Eric said to Ross. "You want to come along?"

"Sure thing," Ross replied before both headed to Eric's unmarked sedan.

It only took a minute to arrive on the scene, and his lousy feeling went into full-blown rage. He'd been searching for this car for days, and now suddenly it's only blocks away from the shots fired at Brad and Finn. Dan's rental car. *Motherfucker.*

"Is that what I think it is?" Ross asked. Ross had spent time helping Eric look into the whereabouts of his former stepfather.

"Yep, it is." *Shit.*

"What's going on, guys?" Clay asked while Sam was in his squad car, no doubt running the license plate, which was necessary for the report, but not for Eric.

When Sam suddenly looked up through the windshield from his notes, Eric knew his friend had come to with the same conclusion: Dan.

It appeared his stepfather just attempted to kill the man Eric loved.

"Get the lab guys down here," he ordered. "I want this vehicle taken in and gone over with a microscope and a Q-Tip. Then I want to know where the bastard is hiding."

"On it, sir," Clay said before walking back to their cruiser.

"You don't think Dan would have done this, do you?" Ross asked.

"I wouldn't put anything past him."

"Hell, the guy used to be a cop."

"Which means he'll know the routine. Our next steps and procedures." That knowledge could make him difficult to find, and even harder to apprehend."

"I'll put an officer on Brad and his grandmother. The bastard won't get anywhere near them," Ross assured.

"Good. Call Northeast and tell them to send a car around and to check on Mrs. Alverez. I'll call them both to explain, so they understand when they show up."

Ross placed his hand on Eric's shoulder and squeezed. "We won't let anything happen to your family."

"Nobody would be able to stop me if it does."

"Remember not to say that in certain company, man. They'll have you talking to the psyche." Ross grinned.

He didn't realize how serious Eric's statement was.

***

Brad stared at the pale moon through their bedroom window. He considered it theirs because he was spending more time at Eric's house than back at his and Grams' apartment. However, he had to admit he preferred to be here as much as Eric wanted him here.

Grams was content having found a close friend in Mrs. Alverez, and he hadn't seen her this hopeful in a long time. You'd think the two of them were planning to take over the world. They sat up until all hours eating and talking. Brad was relieved Grams was next door and had Mrs. Alverez to keep her company. He hadn't been the only one who took Gramps's illness and death hard. They both were moving on from that time, and he wasn't going to allow Dan to ruin the happy they both had found.

More than a week had passed since Brad had been shot at and the missing rental car had turned up. The frustration over finding Dan compounded every day that went by that they didn't find him.

Janet had decided to return to Florida to finalize a few things with her lawyer, taking Miguel and Finn along with her in case Dan got any ideas and attempted to confront her. She wanted to inventory the house, and get a forensic accounting of their bank accounts. Her lawyer had warned her that Dan probably had one or more bank accounts in his own name, where he probably banked all of the money Eric had sent over the years.

The Gates crew had been understanding and helping as much as they could, but until Dan surfaced, there wasn't much they could do.

"Couldn't sleep?" Eric's roughened voice sent chills throughout Brad's body.

"No. I keep expecting Dan to pop out of nowhere, like the boogeyman or something."

Eric's arms tightened around him as Brad's back pressed against the big guy's chest. Their legs were intertwined, and he could feel Eric's cock nestled along his butt cheeks. Even with them lying so closely, it was never enough for Brad. If there were a way for them to be closer, he'd have found it by now. Instead, he pressed himself as much as possible, and once snuggled in, an idea came to him.

"Remember, you said this was an equal relationship and that we were partners," he said.

"Yep, and we are," Eric answered between placing small kisses to the back of Brad's neck.

Although he'd always bottomed, he thought if a part of his body entered Eric's the thrill of being one with him was exciting, and would go beyond any closeness Brad could imagine. "There's something I've never done before but want to try."

Eric slid back a few inches, leaving enough room to turn Brad over onto his back. Those dark eyes looked straight into him, and Brad hoped that by the smile on his face, Eric was on the same wavelength as him.

"Do tell. Something you've never done in the bedroom, I'm guessing." His dark eyebrows raised to almost his hairline. "Am I right?"

"Yeah," Brad said, his enthusiasm bubbling over. "I would love to top you."

Eric's expression heated even more, if that were possible. The palm of his hand brushed across Brad's abdomen and up to his chest, only stopping to squeeze his peaked nipples. Brad's moan echoed through the bedroom as Eric's hand ventured lower until he had it wrapped around Brad's hard cock.

"You want to slide this into me?" he asked while pumping his hand up and down Brad's length.

"Sooo badly," Brad hissed.

Eric leaned down and took Brad's lips in a punishing kiss. Though no part of his mouth had been left unexplored, he still wanted more as he held Eric tight. When Brad broke the kiss, Eric's wet tongue ventured across his jaw and down his throat. Licking and sucking as he went. Brad was sure he'd have a host of hickeys by morning, which sounded perfect. Eric never left any visible when he had his shirt on, but Brad knew they were there and relished Eric's mark on him.

Arching his back, Brad pushed closer to Eric's mouth as his tongue circled his left nipple before sucking it into his hot mouth. He reeled at the sensations and began clawing at the sheets as his desire grew. He heard the unmistakable sound of a cap popping open, but it was swept away on the next wave of pleasure.

Eric continued his journey further down his body, across his stomach, and around his belly button until he was hovering over Brad's throbbing cock.

"For the love of all that's holy, don't stop now," Brad groaned, making his lover chuckle.

Before he had a chance to say another word Eric ran the tip of his tongue from the base of Brad's cock to the tip before swallowing him down in one quick motion. His back bowed and his toes curled at the feel of Eric's wet, hot mouth and wicked tongue, turning him into a writhing mess.

Their moans combined into a hedonistic chorus. Every movement heightened his pleasure and stoked his need. Then suddenly, it all stopped. Eric pulled off and crawled up to the top of the bed.

"Make love to me, babe," he said, and Brad was up on his knees behind Eric so fast he had to blink a few times to clear his vision. Thankfully, he had the presence of mind to slow down. Hurting Eric was the last thing he wanted to do.

The sight of his strong man offering himself proved to be too much. It forced him to pull on his balls to stop himself from coming. Once he felt he was under control again, he fanned his hands over the top of Eric's muscled ass.

"I wasn't joking. I've never topped anyone before," Brad had to warn him. "I'm worried I'll hurt you because of my inexperience."

Eric shifted and leaned back to look at him. "I trust you. I've already prepared myself. All you have to do is slide into me." Yeah, he was going to come before he had a chance to get that far.

Brad reached for the condom, laying on the bedside table and rolled it down his shaft as Eric watched. He never knew how hot that could be. Eric cupped Brad's cheek and said, "I love you."

"I love you, too."

He resumed his position in front of Brad, who had begun running his fingers between his firm cheeks to find his hole already lubed and stretched. He assumed Eric must have done that while Brad was distracted by Eric's talented mouth. Then, Brad remembered the sound of the lid.

He ran the tip of his index finger around Eric's hole, causing the big man to moan and lower his head even further onto the bed. There was no greater invitation, and he accepted. Lining the end of his cock up against Eric's hole had his balls throbbing, making him worry again about how long he might last.

Slowly he pushed forward past the tight ring and didn't stop until his balls rested against Eric's ass. The snug heat pulsed around him, but he held himself still until his lover was ready for him to move. There'd be no rushing this.

Moments later, Eric was pushing back against him, his big hands fisting the sheets as he released a deep groan.

"Move, babe," Eric gasped.

His mind focused on nothing else than bringing Eric pleasure. Brad started slowly with small thrusts in and out, but as he got his rhythm, he adjusted his angle and found Eric's sweet spot.

Brad tried to brush against the gland with every stroke, and between the incredible sensation of his body being inside Eric's and the intense pull of his tight channel, beads of sweat began rolling down Brad's face, but he didn't slow. His fingers dug into Eric's hips, surely leaving bruises behind as Brad increased his pace.

Eric's moans became an endless stream as they merged into a deep rumbling sound coming from his chest. The bedding had been pulled free from the mattress and two pillows laid on the hardwood floor. Reaching up with his right hand, Eric grabbed hold of the headboard, his knuckles turning white as he held on tight.

Brad could feel his balls begin to tingle and knew he was moments away from coming. He released one hip and slid his hand around Eric's body to take hold of his cock, pumping the thick shaft in time with his thrusts.

Eric's body stilled as his cock throbbed in Brad's hand seconds before he hollered and released a stream of come onto the crumpled sheets below. His hole clamped down, pulsing around Brad's cock and pulling his orgasm from his body with mind-numbing speed.

As the last drops were wrenched from his shaking body, Brad collapsed on top of Eric, who supported both their weights before slowly lowering them down onto the mattress. They were gasping for breath, and Brad wasn't sure he could move even if he wanted to.

"Sure you've never done that before?" Eric chuckled, causing Brad to bounce as he laid on his back.

"No, never."

"Feel free to let me know whenever you get the urge again," Eric rasped.

"You got it."

Chapter Fifteen

The next morning Brad arrived early to The Gates for their monthly inventory. Eric had dropped him off on his way to the LAX to pick up his mother. At times, Brad still had to pinch himself to make sure what he felt and what he had been given was real. In his wildest imagination, he never thought he'd ever say he was in love with Eric Meyers, let alone want to build a life with him. And better still, Eric felt the same way about Brad.

Brad waved at a few of the waitstaff on his way to the bar. Most of the employees came in to help with inventory so that they could get it done before The Gates opened. It tended to be a bit crazy for a couple of hours, but the work always managed to get done on time.

After stowing his backpack in one of the lower cupboards, Brad began pulling the bottles down off the shelves and lining them up along the bar top for his counts. The fridges would be next, then the alcohol in the storeroom, along with the kegs.

He rubbed his fingers along one of the scenes carved into the wood hanging around the bar. Finn had told him the story of Saint's mother, how she loved this place back in its heyday, and these carvings. They were unique, and he could appreciate that. The central staircase carving was set behind glass to protect it, and Brad wondered if that was one of Saint's favorites or his mother's.

On his way to the back to collect his inventory sheets, he noticed the smell of smoke getting stronger. When he opened the door to the kitchen, he found flames were shooting out from behind the industrial grill and up the kitchen wall.

A single cook stood fighting them back with a fire extinguisher. Brad opened the kitchen door and yelled, "Fire, fire. Call the fire department."

Without waiting for an answer, he grabbed two more fire extinguishers from the other side of the kitchen, ran over to the fire, pulled the pin, and sprayed. The white powder exploded out of the nozzle as he aimed it at the flames licking up the wall.

He hoped other staff had come in to help, but he was concentrating on keeping the flames at bay, so he wasn't sure. When the first fire extinguisher emptied, he grabbed the second and carried on. By now, black smoke was filling the kitchen, and he was beginning to have a hard time breathing. The thick smoke was becoming overpowering.

A hand grabbed his shoulder, and he turned to find firefighters streaming in through the kitchen door. He handed the extinguisher to the professional and headed out the same door, trying to catch his breath on the way. When he reached the dining room, he kept on going to the front of the building. He needed fresh air desperately.

His white shirt was singed black, and his hands were sore from holding onto the extinguisher so close to the flames. He unlocked the doors and stumbled out into the sunlight. With his hands on his knees, he tried to calm himself to get his breathing under control.

Boots appeared in front of him, followed by a sharp pain to the back of his head. Before he knew what was happening, he was picked up and thrown into the back seat of a car. The tan stone façade of The Gates was the last thing he saw before blacking out.

***

Brad's head was pounding. He felt like he'd gone a few rounds with a prizefighter. Then he remembered the fire and struggled to open his eyes. Was he in the hospital? Light poured in through the slits as he opened one eye and then the other. Definitely not a hospital.

The cold concrete floor he was lying on was dusty, with the odd piece of wood, coffee cups, and other assorted litter piled in a corner. He sat up and his head spun, forcing him to close his eyes once again until the world stopped rolling.

"Easy, that's a pretty good bump you've got on the back of your head," a familiar voice whispered.

Brad turned in the direction that the voice came from to find the last person he'd ever expected: Janet. She knelt beside him and examined his head.

"What's going on? Where are we?"

Janet's expression turned furious. "I'm not familiar with this neighborhood, but we're surrounded by other dilapidated buildings and a few burned-down houses. As for what's going on—revenge, I'm sure."

"What?" That knock on the head made his brain fuzzy.

"Dan has locked us in here."

Brad turned slowly and took a more in-depth look around the space. That's when he noticed the shackles around his and Janet's right legs attaching them to the wall by a thick chain. He looked down at the padlocks holding them captive. The hardened steel would undoubtedly do the job, but he was more interested in the combination tumblers on the underside, along with a slot for a key.

Four tumblers, each with ten digits, roughly ten thousand combinations. Great. "Janet, do you know any of your ex's PINs or favorite numbers?"

Janet leaned back against the concrete wall. "I've already tried every combination I could think of, and nothing works."

"How long has Dan been gone?"

"It's been hours since he brought you in here."

"How did he get you?" Then the realization hit him. "Is Eric all right? He was going to pick you up at the airport."

"I never saw him," she said. "The flight was uneventful, and I was excited to get back to you guys. When I got off the plane, a police officer was waiting for me at the gate. He said that Eric had gotten tied up at the station and that he was there to take me back to your place. Since I'd seen this officer before when he came to the house to tell me he was doing drive-bys, I thought I was safe, so I went with him."

"Wait, didn't Miguel and Finn go with you to Florida?" He couldn't imagine anything getting past Miguel.

"They did. Nice people, those two. However, security had pulled them aside. I don't know why. I was supposed to wait for them, but I was desperate to find a washroom. By the time I'd realized my mistake, it was too late, and the next thing I knew, I was being dragged into this condemned building."

"Condemned?"

"Yes. I saw the notices plastered all over the entrance, or it might have said construction. Chain link fencing surrounds it. I didn't get a good enough look at the street signs, but I do know that there's graffiti covering the old art deco design, and it has many broken windows. Such a shame, it must have been beautiful in its time."

"Did you happen to notice how tall the building was?" Maybe with more of a description, he could figure out where they were.

"I think five stories, but it's a long building and white if I had to guess. The sun was in my eyes."

Brad stood up to take a better look around. Down a hallway, the sun shined in, and he could see shadows of prison bars and more graffiti. He could hear birds singing as well as traffic on what he assumed was a freeway. He noticed the wire mesh covering the broken windows and began taking a closer look at the graffiti.

Growing up in DTLA in a working-class neighborhood, Brad knew some of the taggers and gangs in different areas of the city. Many would mark their turf that way to warn off nonmembers or rival gangs from being found in the wrong neighborhood. He'd also done a bit of urban exploration in his time.

Brad scanned the walls as far as he could see, which wasn't much thanks to his chain. He was about to give up when he saw it: the LH in stylized writing surrounded by a blue crest. Damnit, he knew exactly where they were, and it didn't make him feel any better.

"Janet, I think I know where we are."

She stood and joined him, dragging her chain behind her. "Where?"

"Lincoln Heights. More specifically, Lincoln Heights Jail." They'd been chained in a somewhat infamous building that had been closed in 1965. Where were the security guards? He had run into one when he'd been exploring years ago.

The Zoot Suit Riots took place in this area, and many of the participants had been jailed inside this building. Al Capone spent a night here, among other mobsters and celebrities of the golden age of Hollywood. This was also the place where several LAPD officers had beaten seven civilians on what was called Bloody Christmas. Apparently, it was an utterly unprovoked attack that happened on December twenty-fifth in the early fifties.

He was almost positive that one of the many reasons Dan had brought them here was also the jail's not-so-shining history of having a disproportionate number of inmates arrested as being suspected of being gay.

"Lincoln Heights Jail," Janet repeated. "Where have I heard that name before...?"

Brad went over to the concrete wall and pulled on the eye bolt securing his chain to the stone. The bolts appeared to be as old as the building and painted several times over the years. It made him think that perhaps the metal or concrete had weakened over time, considering they seemed original. When he couldn't get it to budge, he tried Janet's with much the same result.

Frustrated, he sat back down on the ground and took a closer look at the padlock.

"I remember where I've heard the name of this jail before," Janet said, half to herself. "Dan's grandfather used to work here back in the forties or fifties. He used to talk about it all the time. Eventually, I stopped listening to his stories of how he came from a long line of policing beginning right here."

"That explains a lot. This place represents the beginning of his not-so-illustrious line." Brad thought it was likely Dan's grandfather was involved in the illegal goings-on in Lincoln Heights Jail. The apple didn't fall far from the tree.

"I'm so sorry to have gotten you into this. If I had known what was going on, I could have stopped it from happening," Janet said. "Maybe I wasn't paying close enough attention."

Brad scooched over to sit beside Janet and took her into his arms for a hug. "None of this is your fault. Dan was skilled at hiding his crazy. When he lost control of you and Eric, he snapped and the crazy took over. I doubt no matter how hard you watched him, he would have never let it slip. I know a few people like that—sociopaths."

She laid her head on his shoulder and let the tears fall. Brad held her for as long as she needed. This woman had been exceptionally kind and supportive of his and Eric's relationship and welcomed him into her family. He'd take on Dan, and whoever was working with him before Brad ever let something happen to her.

***

Eric stood in the center of the station as officers and volunteers hustled around him. Little did they know he was on the hunt for the person involved in the kidnapping of his mother and Brad. They had a dirty cop among them.

Ross was busy checking files and schedules while Sam and Clay kept themselves looking busy searching for anything out of the ordinary. Eric knew it wasn't one of those three. He'd known Ross for over a decade and knew the man liked his mom and Brad. Clay had been by Sam's side since seven this morning.

Whoever the officer was had to have been familiar to his mother or she wouldn't have left with them. When Miguel and Finn made it past airport security, she was already gone. They'd asked every member of the airport and auto rental staff, and one person remembered a man in an LAPD uniform escorting a lady matching her description by the arm.

That narrowed it down somewhat. The witness described him as having short blond hair and glasses. There were three men in Eric's unit matching that description who'd spent time watching over his loved ones. Two had recently come on shift, which means they'd been able to go to LAX this morning.

At shift changeover, Eric had purposely asked a team of officers to help in the search while others worked the streets looking for any lead that would take him to the people he loved. Dan had no idea who he was messing with.

The constant buzz of conversations filled the air around him. However, all of his attention remained on the two men in question. Both were at their desks, one on the station computer system and the other working with two other officers laying out maps and marking off areas that had already come up with no sign of them.

His heart was aching, his stress was off the charts, and his patience was wearing thin. Eric felt tempted to take both of them into separate interrogation rooms, and sweat a confession out of whoever took his family.

Clay was making the rounds with coffee, behaving like a concerned rookie overwhelmed by the situation. He was pulling it off masterfully, with his downcast eyes and stumbling over his words. No one paid much attention to him. He was heading in Officer Jack Henderson's direction, coffee pot in hand.

Henderson had stopped working on his computer and was now holding his cellphone. Clay meandered between desks, striking up short conversations, and then moving on. When he reached one of the two suspects, he did something Eric hadn't seen coming. He poured the coffee onto Henderson's lap, making the man holler, drop his cellphone, and stand up, brushing off the front of his soaked uniform.

"I'm so sorry, Henderson," Clay said. "I must have tripped or something."

"You idiot. Look what you've done to my clothing. Rookies are useless."

"Again, I'm sorry. Do you want me to help clean your pants in the bathroom?"

Henderson reared back so fast the Eric thought he was going to fall over his chair. "I don't need your help. Stay the fuck away from me," he said before storming out.

Clay picked the coffee pot up off the floor and headed in Eric's direction. Sam was making his way out the door, following Henderson.

"Could I speak with you, sir?" Clay asked as he came to stand in front of him, keeping the charade going strong.

"Sure. Follow me." Eric had seen what Clay had done.

Once the door to his office was closed, Clay pulled out Henderson's cell phone.

"Now let's see what had him so distracted," Eric said as he brought the screen to life.

Eric went straight to the call log. None of the recent numbers had a name attached to them, but when he went further back, he found what he suspected.

"Bring Henderson to me."

Clay left, and Eric sat behind his desk. He couldn't disguise his anger for the sake of questioning Henderson and gave up trying. The officer was a twenty-year veteran of the force. How he'd gotten mixed up with Dan was a question mark.

There was a knock on his door, and he hollered for them to enter. Henderson, followed by Sam and Clay, walked in.

"Close the door," he ordered.

Henderson looked nervous, and he had a reason to be. "You needed to speak with me?"

Eric placed Henderson's phone onto the top of his desk and waited. He looked down at his phone and back up at Eric. "Why do you have my phone?"

"You must've dropped it on the floor. Have a seat, Henderson."

The man didn't even argue, making Eric suspect that he already knew he was caught.

"Wasn't sure whose phone it was and went scrolling around. Was damn surprised to see there's a call from the phone number of a man we've been searching for who is the prime suspect in a double kidnapping." Eric stood and circled to the front of his desk to stand directly in front of Henderson. "Can you tell me why you have Dan Smith's number on your phone?"

Henderson began to squirm in his chair, looking anywhere other than at Eric. "Remove your gun slowly with your index finger and your thumb and place it on my desk."

Both Sam and Clay took a step forward to make sure the disgraced officer didn't get any stupid ideas. Once they'd removed the gun from his possession, Eric said, "I'm placing you under arrest for violating California Criminal Code section two-zero-seven-A, aggravated kidnapping. You have the right to remain silent. Anything you say can and will be used against you in a court of law. You have the right to an attorney. If you can't afford an attorney, one will be provided to you. Do you understand your rights?"

Henderson nodded and Eric said, "You have to provide verbal acknowledgment."

"I understand my rights," Henderson ground out.

"The way I see it," Eric stated, "you're in way over your head. We have a witness who can place you at the airport taking Janet Meyers away this morning. We could bring her to ID you in a lineup, but that would take the time that my mother and Bradley don't have. Before you become an accomplice to a double murder, tell me where they are." Even saying the words made Eric sick, but he had to impress the gravity of the situation on Henderson.

The officer looked from Clay to Sam as if they were magically going to tell him what to do.

"Look at me. You're a dirty cop, and the time has come to try to save yourself from death row. I promise you if one hair on either of their heads is touched, you'll never have to worry about making it to court. A dirty cop put in gen pop, how long do you think you would last?"

Eric was leaning over Henderson, making him have to stretch his neck back to look at him. He could see the fear written all over his face and almost hear the sound of his racing heart. Eric laid it all out, and if Henderson thought he was bluffing, he was in for a nasty surprise.

"Cuff him," he ordered as Ross walked into the office, holding a piece of paper.

He handed the paper to Eric and gave Henderson a death glare. "Seems somebody won the lottery. With all these deposits, it looks like you were getting paid piecemeal. You completed a task, Dan gave you money, and on it went. The last deposit took place at noon today."

"You can't dig into my bank records without my authorization," Henderson complained while Sam secured his cuffs. "I have rights."

"You'd be surprised how fast you can get a warrant when lives are at stake," Ross growled while waving the warrant in the air.

Henderson didn't say another word, and Eric figured he'd let him sit in a cell and think about it while they continued to search. "Take him to holding."

They pulled him out of the chair by his arms and led him to the door. "Wait," Henderson called. "I'll tell you what I know. I want it on the record I helped."

Eric nodded. "Start by telling me where I can find my family."

Chapter Sixteen

Brad suspected Dan would be returning soon since night had fallen. They had to get free before that happened, or he doubted either of them would make it out of this building alive.

Janet was still leaning against the cold wall, her knees pulled up tight to her body, and her face lowered. The poor woman was dealing with a lot, so he left her in peace while he thought through his limited options.

He had to get these padlocks off somehow so they could make a run for safety. Brad was positive that Eric was turning the city upside down searching for them, but that help could come too late.

If I had my lock-pick tools, I'd already have us free.

"Shit," he exclaimed while reaching back to make sure he still had his wallet. Brad had almost forgotten about the tools he'd stitched into the leather.

"What's wrong?" Janet asked, coming closer to him. "Did you hear something?" She scanned the darkening halls. Streetlights were beginning to turn on, casting an eerie glow across the interior.

Even when he'd been exploring this jail as a teenager, Brad didn't dare stay after dark. There were one too many ghost stories of former prisoners walking these halls. He pulled out his wallet and opened it up. To anyone else, there was no visible alterations to the wallet, unless you knew where to look.

A single thread poked out from underneath the clear plastic credit card holders. He pushed the plastic aside and pulled on the string until a one-inch opening appeared on the seam. Sticking his fingers inside, he'd never been happier to feel the thin metal picks in his life.

Brad pulled them out one at a time until all three were lying on the concrete. He shoved his wallet back into the back pocket of his jeans and went to work.

"What are those?" Janet asked.

Shit. Great time to have your new mother-in-law find out about your past profession.

"They're lock picks," he explained. "I forgot I had them."

"Lock picks? We will have to have a long talk after this is over, young man," she warned. "Though I am thrilled you have them."

"Yes, ma'am," Brad mumbled while he continued to work on the keyhole on the bottom of the padlock. Hopefully there'd be time for explaining later.

He was out of practice, and it took him a couple of minutes to make the lock click open. Brad remove the shackle from around his ankle then went to work on Janet's lock. Using the same twist, push, and turn that'd worked on his lock earned him another click, and they were free, at least from the chains. Now they needed to make it out of the building before Dan realized they were gone.

"Let's get out of here," Brad said.

"Right behind you, dear."

As they walked, they tried to stay as quiet as possible to keep Dan from hearing where they were going. Brad was wracking his brain, trying to remember anything from his previous visit to the jail that could help them, but he was drawing a blank. He hoped something would come to him eventually.

They continued down a long, dark hall, past a row of cells, some with their doors open, others still locked tight. When they came to an end, Brad took a look out one of the three windows to get a better idea of which floor they were one. His best guess put them on the fourth floor, which meant they had a long way to go before walking out the front door.

Brad opened a metal door off to the side, revealing a set of stairs. Halleluiah. "Let's try these and see how far down we can get."

Janet nodded as Brad stuck a piece of broken concrete against the door to hold it open. They'd have to use what little light was shining in from the moon and streetlights to find their way. He took Janet's hand, not wanting to lose her in the darkness, as well as needing a bit of reassurance himself.

"You're doing great, Brad," Janet said as she placed a comforting hand on his shoulder. "I trust you to get us out of here."

He sucked in a deep breath and took the first step. Carefully, they inched their way down the stairwell. With every step, his hopes increased that they'd make it out of here without any run-ins—at least until he heard the footsteps coming from below them.

Heavy boots, by the amount of noise they were making. Not certain who was coming, they sure as hell weren't going to stick around to find out. On the next landing, Brad took the exit onto the third floor, and quickly ran to the next bisecting hallway, rounded the corner, and flattened their backs against the wall. His heart was racing

The footsteps kept coming ever closer, amplified in the empty building until Brad was sure they were coming to the third-floor landing. He held his breath and waited, but thankfully, the steps continued up the stairs. It wouldn't be long before Dan discovered they were missing. Brad had to find another staircase.

"We have to move," he whispered to Janet. "Stay right behind me."

Brad headed in the opposite direction of the stairwell they'd been using. He thought he remembered another staircase on the other end of the building. They came upon what must have been solitary confinement. The bars on the doors were covered, hiding the cells inside.

"Wait, I remember this," Brad said as he stopped in the middle of the hallway. "If I'm right, there's a staff room over here to the right."

He turned in that direction, and roughly thirty feet away, they found the door he'd been remembering. Brad opened it, and sure enough, he'd been right. A few pieces of wood from the broken chairs were piled in the corners. Graffiti covered the walls, and what looked like deteriorating sheetrock exposed the concrete blocks.

The sound of doors slamming made them both jump. The following anger-filled scream assured him that their escape was no longer a secret. Janet inched closer to Brad. He took her hand and led her to the far side of the room and another open doorway.

"This leads down to the second floor to what I think was a kitchen at one time," he whispered. "It's going to be pitch dark. Don't worry. I'll make sure you don't fall."

Janet looked determined. "That bastard isn't going to catch us," she said before picking up a piece of wood roughly two feet long. She meant business, and now Brad knew where Eric got his strength from.

They stepped into the darkness. Using his hands and feet, he felt his way down the dark staircase, inching one foot forward at a time until he could feel the edge of the stair they were on. Janet clung to his back. The length of wood she'd brought along was digging into his skin. He wasn't about to mention it, especially if the makeshift weapon made her feel safer.

Behind them, he could hear cell doors slamming shut and muffled words. Dan was still too far away for him to make out what he was saying. Thank God.

He sighed in relief when they made it to the landing between floor three and two. They were halfway down. Turning the corner to reach the second set of stairs that would take them to the next level, Brad heard something wholly unexpected and frightening at the same time. Panting.

Janet's fingers held on a little tighter as he inched his foot forward, bumping into something that was moving. He heard claws scraping against the floor as it moved. What the hell else was going to happen to them, a freak earthquake?

Whatever it was, it began sniffing his legs, and Brad took the chance of lower his left hand to show he wasn't a threat. Seconds later, a warm, wet, canine tongue licked his hand and brushed up against his legs for more attention.

"It's a dog," he whispered to Janet. "It's friendly. Keep going."

They continued with their new companion at their sides until they came to another door. Brad slowly opened it and took a look out down the new set of hallways. This place was a maze. The coast was clear, so he opened the door wide and led Janet and what turned out to be a black lab from the stairwell.

Brad didn't have time to check out the dog. They had to keep moving. Something crashed on the floor above them, making the dog bark, and they quickened their pace. He wasn't sure which way to go and decided one way was as good as another and chose left. The dog stayed with them, and he only hoped Dan didn't follow the barks.

They turned down one hallway after another, and as Brad turned, they passed a large open room, and what he thought looked like the ring of an old basketball hoop. Beyond that, they ran straight into the security guards.

Only they'd be of no help.

At the sight of the two bodies, Janet screamed. He couldn't blame her. Who runs into a couple of dead bodies and takes it in stride? *Shit.* Dan had to've heard Janet.

The dog padded over to one of the security guards, sniffed him, and whined. Brad had a sick feeling that the person had been the dog's owner. Fucking Dan.

"I'm sorry, I shouldn't have screamed," Janet muttered

"It's okay. We've gotta move faster."

Now that they had the streetlights glowing in from the windows, they picked up speed. No longer concerned about being overheard, they raced to get out before Dan caught up to them. Brad spotted an open door hiding a staircase. This one wasn't as wide as the others but was still going down, so they took it.

Brad caught hold of Janet as she missed a step and lunged forward. He put his left arm around her waist, feeling the familiar zing of pain, and kept going.

More cursing and crashing came from above them, which meant at least they were still ahead of Dan.

When they reached the first floor, Brad would have kissed the ground if he'd had time, he was so relieved. They came out into what looks to be a set of old offices. Most of the walls were destroyed, allowing him to see through to the far end of the building.

As he was considering which way to go, Dan came running into view at the same end of the building. The dog started barking. Dan's eyes were blown wide as if he was on something. The moment Dan saw them, he raised his gun.

Brad grabbed hold of Janet and raced in the other direction, Janet on one side, the dog on the other. Room after room, the sound of gunshots and bullets ricocheting off the walls made them move even faster than even he thought he could run.

"There has to be an exit somewhere," Brad said. "Or I'll take a hole in the wall. Anything." Shit, they were out of time.

The dog barked at them as if leading the way. Hell, Brad didn't have any better ideas, so he followed. After two more turns, through a door and over more debris, the three of them came to an exterior wall. Vines were growing in from top to bottom like he'd see on some fancy houses, with big flowers and leaves. It was too pretty to be here.

The dog went to the far end and disappeared into the greenery. Brad ran over and pulled the vines aside, revealing what he'd been praying for, a hole in the concrete. The hole must have been one of the ways urban explorers got in. Years ago, he'd used the same method in a different part of the facility.

"Go," Brad urged Janet taking her piece of lumber and almost pushing her through. He had to get her out of here.

When she'd made it to the other side, his relief was instant but short-lived.

"Where the fuck do you think you're going?" Dan growled from behind him while grabbing onto Brad's foot.

He looked out at Janet and yelled, "Run," before being pulled back inside.

Brad firmed his grip on the piece of wood still in his hands. He'd be damned if he'd go easily. The moment his arms cleared the hole, Brad swung the wood like a bat connecting with the side of Dan's head, dropping him to the ground. The only problem with that was the bastard fell in front of the hole.

With his only escape route blocked, he took off once again into the bowels of the jail, searching for another way out. Brad didn't know how long Dan would be down, so he ran straight back to get as far away as possible.

All too soon, he could hear Dan yelling for him to give up. Every door he checked went nowhere, and there was no way in hell he was going back up. He turned left again and straight into a large room with no other doors. When he turned around, Dan, blood dripping down from the side of his head, was standing only a few feet away from him, gun raised and pointed at his chest.

Brad backed into the room, trying to put some distance between them, though he was now trapped in this room with the asshole.

"Thought you could get away from me," Dan growled. "You don't know who you are dealing with. I'll catch up to my dear wife after I've dealt with you."

"Leave her alone. None of this is her fault." Brad accepted he might not make it out of here, but he needed to give Janet time to get away. "Why are you doing this?"

If a look could kill, Brad would be lying on the ground. "Because of you. He'd never tried this bullshit before you. I'd set up my entire life, and now it's gone. I could gamble all I wanted, and that fool,

Eric, kept sending money. I had him convinced his mother was sick. He never pushed back and did what he was told."

"You could have had a good life with an amazing wife and son."

"Yeah, the fag. No fucking way," He looked around the room. "My grandfather served in this building. My dad told me stories about the good old days when his dad could pull anyone suspected of being like you off the streets, rough them up, and throw them in a cell."

"Grade A cop, right there."

Dan jammed the gun forward into Brad's face. "Don't you say a single derogatory word about him. My grandfather and his fellow officers did what they had to do to keep that shit away from our children."

Brad was staring down the barrel of a gun. It had been a wild ride these past few months; he'd miss his Grams and Eric. Oh, how he'd miss that man. He closed his eyes and waited. He'd be dead before he heard the gunfire.

Instead, Dan punched him in the jaw, causing Brad to fly backward and against the stone wall. His feet went out from under him, and he slid down and slumped against the wall. Everything was fuzzy. He couldn't get his eyesight to clear, making him wonder if the bastard had hit him with his fist or the gun.

A vicious growl tore through the room as something black attacked Dan. His screams stopped at the sound of a gunshot. Brad tried blinking and shaking his sore head, but his sight wouldn't clear. He heard the dog whine in pain, and he tried to crawl over in its direction.

"Fucking dog," Dan bellowed. "I should have killed it when I shot its owner."

"Leave him alone," Brad yelled as his outstretched hand finally felt the dog's fur. He quickly ran his hands over the dog. He was still breathing.

"Time to end this. I'll make sure to give your regards to Janet."

Brad looked in Dan's direction, and even though he couldn't see him clearly, the glint of metal confirmed his gun was pointed in Brad's direction once again. He leaned down over the dog, knowing it wouldn't help in the end.

He waited, but nothing happened. The asshole had to be drawing this out in some sick kind of pleasure. When he looked up, Brad wasn't sure what he was seeing, but what appeared to be shadows stood around the room.

"Help me," Brad cried out, and the shadows moved closer.

Oddly, Dan hadn't moved, except to point the gun in a totally different direction.

"What the fuck?" Dan growled and began firing off rounds at the shadows.

Bullets ricochet off the stone walls, and Brad dove back down over the dog. Undoubtedly, both of them were going to get hit by one of those bullets, but the searing pain never came. When the noise stopped, Brad opened his eyes, still unable to make out much. He slowly lifted his head and turned in the direction he'd last seen Dan standing to find him lying on the ground unmoving.

The bastard must have shot himself. The shadows were gone, Brad and his new friend were alone. His head was pounding, and his vision began to dim. Brad struggled to stay awake. He had to get the dog some help, but it was a lost cause as his head lowered back down onto the dog's soft fur. The poor dog's labored breaths broke his heart.

"Thank you for trying to save me. You're a good boy."

The last thing he heard was the dog's tail hitting the ground as it wagged, and Brad vaguely wondered if he'd see his Gramps again before the world went dark.

Chapter Seventeen

The light burned his eyes every time he tried to open them.

"Turn off the light," a familiar voice said, "and get the doctor."

"Eric?"

"Hey, babe. I'm right beside you. Hold on, and we'll get it dark in here."

He had to ask because it felt almost impossible. "I'm alive?"

Warm hands cupped his face, and soon he felt those achingly familiar soft lips covering his. Brad melted at the touch he'd thought he'd never feel again.

Eric pulled back and said, "You are very much alive, thank God."

"What about Janet and the dog? There was a dog that attacked Dan. The bastard shot the dog."

"Easy. Mom is fine and resting at home, and as for the dog, we found you lying over him. He's at the vet undergoing surgery to try to save his back leg."

"Is that where he was shot? I couldn't see a thing," Brad muttered as he tried reopening his eyes. The glaring light was mercifully gone, and though he was still in pain, he was able to keep them open this time.

His surroundings still looked fuzzy, but he wasn't dead. It looked like he was in a hospital, which, of course, made sense.

"How long have I been out?"

"About four hours. We'd stormed the building and were searching for you when we heard the gunfire. You were unconscious when I found you. Dan is dead from multiple gunshot wounds."

"He was shooting at the shadows. Bullets were flying all over the room." Brad searched his body but felt no pain other than in his head and jaw. "I wasn't shot?"

Eric gently ran his fingers through Brad's hair. "Nope. The crazy bastard went over the edge. Shooting at the walls. Fuck, by some miracle, you weren't hit."

"For real, there were shadows in the shape of men, but that's all I could see with my vision screwed up."

"Other than the security guards, we found no one else in the building, sweetheart. We're going to get the doctor in here so he can check on your eyes."

When Eric made to leave, Brad refused to release his hand. "Don't leave." He was freaked out and having trouble seeing anything properly.

"Okay, Bradley. I'm here, babe, and I won't leave your side. I may never let you out of my sight again after this."

"No more stepfathers for you. Tell your mom," Brad tried to joke but it only made him groan in pain as his head shook.

"I love you, Bradley."

That helped. "I love you, Eric."

"How about we shack up?"

"Shack up? Are you suggesting we live in sin?" He smiled even though it hurt like hell

"No. We've got to preserve your reputation. How about we get married and make the whole thing legal?"

Brad was shocked into silence. They'd known each other for four months. What if Eric changed his mind? What if Brad changed his mind? The odds of that happening were slim to none. He loved Eric and wanted to build a life with him.

"Yeah."

"Yeah?" Eric asked.

"Yeah." Those soft lips kissed him again as the door opened to his room.

"Hello, I'm Doctor Currie. It's good to see you awake."

Eric backed off a few steps but never released Brad's hand. Their connection had been strong since the beginning, and had grown over time.

Absolutely, he would marry Eric.

Maybe not tomorrow, but it would happen.

***

Three months later

"I now pronounce you husband and husband."

The small group assembled cheered as the grooms kissed for the first time as a married couple. Janet, Grams, and Mrs. Alverez dabbed their tears with tissues and threw birdseed at the happy couple. The crew from The Gates had shut down the dining room for the day so that they all could attend. Sam and Joey had invited Clay, and Miguel's older brother, Carlos, who'd arrived this morning and was staying at The Gates temporarily.

Finn and Miguel walked back down the aisle in their matching tuxedos.

Brad looked into Eric's eyes and said, "Soon it'll be our turn."

"I'm going to hold you to that," Eric said before kissing the side of Brad's face jarring his sunglasses.

Eric quickly put them back in place, protecting Brad's sensitive eyes. Though his eyesight had been improving, it still wasn't good enough to go back to work, and bright lights were a problem. However, it was a small price to pay. He was here, in his and Eric's backyard, watching two of their friends get married surrounded by family and more friends.

Brad lowered his hand and brushed it over Jerry, their new dog. Well, a new-old dog with three legs. The dog who had protected Brad had lost one of his back legs trying to keep Brad safe. The least he could do was give the sweet boy a home and a name. In truth, he'd demanded they bring him home, but Eric was a quick sale.

Jerry's tail wagged, and he took off running after Mrs. Alverez's dog. Jerry's three legs worked as well as four, and when the children threw balls his way, nothing stopped him from trying to field them. Brad didn't think Jerry paid attention to the difference, if he even noticed it.

Eric wrapped his arms around Brad's waist from behind and kissed the top of his head. "This is the life, babe."

"You got that right."

This was the life.

Brad's new life with Captain Eric Meyers.

They'd earned every minute of it.

ABOUT THE AUTHOR

M. Tasia lives in a small town in Ontario, Canada. She's a member of the Romance Writers of America, and its Rainbow Romance Writers and Toronto Romance Writers chapters. Michelle is a dedicated people-watcher, lover of romance novels, '80s rock, and happy endings. Also, she's the mother of two wonderful girls, wife to a great husband, and a new grandmother, as well as servant to two spoiled furry children who don't seem to realize that they're actually cats.

Michelle writes contemporary and paranormal romance, and she believes love should be celebrated. After all, everybody needs a little romance, excitement, intrigue, and passion in their lives.

Connect with Michelle:

mtasiabooks.com

facebook.com/mtasiabooks

twitter.com/mtasiaauthor

instagram.com/m.tasia.author/

www.BOROUGHSPUBLISHINGGROUP.com

If you enjoyed this book, please write a review. Our authors appreciate the feedback, and it helps future readers find books they love. We welcome your comments and invite you to send them to info@boroughspublishinggroup.com. Follow us on Facebook, Twitter and Instagram, and be sure to sign up for our newsletter for surprises and new releases from your favorite authors.

Are you an aspiring writer? Check out www.boroughspublishinggroup.com/submit and see if we can help you make your dreams come true.

www.ingramcontent.com/pod-product-compliance
Lightning Source LLC
Chambersburg PA
CBHW021116130626
46554CB00002B/726